LITTLE
— by —
LITTLE

A Writer's Education

JEAN LITTLE

**VIKING
KESTREL**

VIKING KESTREL

Penguin Books Canada Ltd, 2801 John Street, Markham,
Ontario, Canada L3R 1B4
Penguin Books Ltd, 27 Wrights Lane, London W8 5TZ
(Publishing & Editorial) and Harmondsworth, Middle-
sex, England (Distribution & Warehouse)
Viking Penguin Inc., 40 West 23rd Street, New York,
New York 10010, U.S.A.
Penguin Books Australia Ltd, Ringwood, Victoria,
Australia
Penguin Books (N.Z.) Ltd, 182-190 Wairau Road, Auck-
land 10, New Zealand

First published by Penguin Books Canada Limited, 1987

Copyright© Jean Little, 1987

Printed in Canada

Canadian Cataloguing in Publication Data

Little, Jean, 1932-
Little by Little

ISBN 0-670-81649-3

1. Little, Jean, 1932-   . 2. Novelists, Canadian (English)
— 20th century — Biography — Juvenile literature.
*3. Blind — Canada — Biography — Juvenile literature.
I. Title.

PS8523.I87Z53 1987   jC813'.54   C87-093540-2
PR9199.3.L57Z47 1987

for Mother

with my love and gratitude

"For your most comfortable hand
Which led me through the uneven land"

— Robert Louis Stevenson

and for Jamie, Hugh and Pat

My thanks to Michelle Kelly and Susan Outram, who assisted me in the research for this book.

AUTHOR'S NOTE

When I was a child, I refused to read a "blue card book." The blue cards were in the pockets in the backs of the non-fiction books in the Guelph Public Library. I liked stories better than facts. So as I began telling the story of my life, in spite of myself, it turned into a tale compounded of both truth and imagination. Although everything that happens in these pages has truth in it, not every word is based on fact. I took my memories and rearranged them, filling in details as I went along. I do not really remember every word that I or others said so long ago. I do, however, know exactly how it felt and what we were likely to have said. If I had included all the background material of which I was then ignorant, this might have turned into a full scale, factual autobiography. I could not let that happen. The child I was would never have forgiven me.

If you find yourself portrayed inaccurately in these pages, remember that memory — yours as well as mine — is a chancy thing and not to be trusted. I have tried to write faithfully of my life as it seemed to me. If you have a different story to tell, go right ahead. I would love to read your version.

"You can't climb up here," Marilyn Dickson said.
"You're not allowed."

I stood at the foot of the banyan tree, the smooth
bark pressing against my palms and stared up at her.
She seemed proud and powerful sitting astride the
high branch. The strip of white flannel that her
mother had wrapped around her neck to ward off a
sore throat kept her head stiffly erect. Something
about the way she gazed loftily down reminded me of
a queen. What she had just said, though, made no
sense. Of course I could climb up there. The banyan
tree did not belong to the Dicksons.

I started to tell her so and then stopped. She was
clearly annoyed over something. If I made her mad-
der, she might stamp off into her house and leave me
with nobody to play with.

When Marilyn and her older brother Ronnie had
come across the lawn between our houses to call for
me and my brothers, she had meant the five of us to
take up the Robin Hood game we had been playing
before dinner. The other four had gone on outside,
leaving me to finish my second helping of lemon
snow pudding. I had come out to find Marilyn all by
herself in the huge tree.

I listened. Ronnie and my brothers, Jamie and
Hugh, were playing soldiers with a bunch of
Taiwanese friends. I could hear them shouting orders
in staccato Chinese from the street outside the compound gate.

"We're playing army," Jamie had probably said. "We don't need a Maid Marian. Go play with Jean." Hugh, Ronnie and the Taiwanese boys would have laughed like anything. Boys were so mean.

Since Jamie had gotten that Robin Hood book for Christmas, acting out Robin's adventures had become our favourite game. Eight-year-old Jamie was Robin, of course, since he was the oldest and could read the book. Ronnie and Hugh, who was only three, were Will Scarlet, Little John and the Sheriff of Nottingham. I was graciously permitted to be Friar Tuck and the entire outlaw band. But Marilyn was chosen to play Maid Marian every single time.

"Why do you always pick her?" I had asked.

Jamie had shown me the illustrations.

"Maid Marian has to have curly hair," he said. "Yours is straight. Besides, Marilyn sounds like Marian."

I was getting sick and tired of Sherwood Forest.

They would never let us play soldiers, though. I'd have to think up a new game, one so good that Marilyn would not be able to resist joining in. I thought fast.

"Let's play my doll is Moses in the bulrushes," I suggested. "We can pretend to go to the river to bathe and discover him. You be his sister Miriam and I'll be Pharoah's daughter."

"I said you can't climb up here," Marilyn repeated as though I had not spoken.

"I can so," I snapped, craning my neck back to glare up at her.

"No. You're not allowed."

That was crazy. I had climbed this very tree often before and my parents had watched me do it. It was the best tree for climbing in the whole compound where our missionary families lived.

"Who says I'm not?" I challenged.

Marilyn shot back the answer so fast that I knew she had been hoping for that very question.

"My mother. She told me not to let you do anything dangerous because you have bad eyes. Climbing trees is dangerous so you can't do it anymore."

Bad eyes! What did that mean?

I longed to yell back at her that it was a lie, but I was not absolutely sure. After all, when Dad had shown us Taiwan on the globe during dinner, hadn't I had to peer at it longer and more closely than the others before I at last spotted that tiny orange sliver of an island off the coast of China?

I also had to hold Jamie's battered copy of *The Adventures of Robin Hood* up so close that my nose brushed the page before I could clearly distinguish Maid Marian's curls.

And when a rickshaw man came padding down the road from the train station and halted at the compound gate, Hugh could tell at a glance that the passenger climbing down was Aunt Gretta. I couldn't. I did not know who it was until I heard her voice or saw the way she moved.

So perhaps my eyes were a bit different.

They weren't "bad," though. Children could be bad. But not eyes. Mrs. Dickson must have made a mistake. Or Marilyn had invented the whole thing.

"I do *not* have Bad Eyes," I told her defiantly. "If your mother said that, she's wrong. My mother never said so and *my* mother is a doctor so she'd know. My father is a doctor, too, and he never said so, either. They both said I can climb any tree I like."

That was not true, but I was positive that if I had asked, they would have said those very words. It came to the same thing.

Running out of breath and patience, I started getting myself up to the lowest thick branch.

Marilyn knew I was lying. Not only that, I was insulting her mother. Her temper blazed.

"*No!*" she shrieked, coming down the tree very fast. She was enjoying herself now. "You do so have bad eyes. My mother said!"

I was furious. I was also a little frightened. There was only one way to settle it. I turned and headed for my house. Marilyn ran to catch up. We crossed the wide verandah and rushed in through the big front door.

Where was Mother? Halfway down the wide hall that divided the house, I halted and called her. Perhaps she heard the panic in my voice. She came at once through the living-room door on my right. Seeing me apparently unharmed, she stopped and smiled down at me.

"What is it, Jean?" she asked in a quiet, calming voice.

"Marilyn says her mother says I have bad eyes," I burst out, my words sputtering in their rush to get said. "She says I can't climb the tree because it's dangerous if you have bad eyes. I don't have them, do I? I can climb the tree, can't I?"

Mother did not hesitate. I can still hear the words that set my world turning on its axis again.

"You do have bad eyes," she said, "but you go right ahead and climb the tree."

Marilyn and I faced each other.

"See!" we chorused. "I told you so."

All the way back outside, we wrangled over who had been proved right. As far as I was concerned, it was crystal clear. I could climb the tree, couldn't I? Reaching the bottom of the verandah steps, I made a dash for the banyan tree. Marilyn flew after me, but to my intense satisfaction, I beat her by several seconds.

As I wriggled up onto the lowest branch, I felt victorious. Yet under my triumph, I was turning over the new knowledge. I did have bad eyes. As I groped for the next handhold, I wondered what that meant. It couldn't be anything very alarming. Mother had not sounded worried. Her hand on my shoulder had stayed steady.

Then my fingers found a crevice they could hook into. Marilyn was right behind me. I pulled myself up, swung my leg over the next branch, panted heavily and flung my body upwards. There was a sickening moment when I felt myself slipping. But only a moment. Then I was astride a thick, trustworthy limb and laughing down at Marilyn. In three seconds she would be level with me. I knew I would not have long to gloat. I leaned down and stuck out my tongue at her, while I had the chance. "I can climb trees better than you can," I mocked, "Who says I have bad eyes?"

Marilyn was too intent on catching up to me to waste breath replying. But inside, I knew the answer. My mother had said so. That made it true. Even though I did not understand it, even though I denied it, even though they seemed to work perfectly well to me, my eyes were "bad."

I had no time to think about it right now, though. Marilyn was trying to push past me. I shoved her back down with one foot and started feeling around for another handhold. Whether I ever got there or not, I was heading for the top of the tree.

❧ 2 ❧

Grandma sat on the piano stool, her hands flying up and down the long row of black and white keys. Hugh and I stood watching her, fascinated by the impossible speed at which her fingers rippled up and down the keyboard. The cascading notes, sweeping from bass to treble and back again, impressed us immensely. Occasional discords did not matter. The dash and noise of her performance were so satisfying.

Grandma taught piano and directed choirs at the mission schools. When adults gathered at our house in the evenings, after we were in bed, I often went to sleep to the sound of her music floating up through the warm, fragrant darkness.

She played proper pieces sometimes, but I preferred this bunch of wild arpeggios. I could tell that Grandma revelled in doing them for us. She always finished by playing a resounding chord. Then she would turn to bask in our open admiration. Grandma relished an audience.

I liked to play the piano, too, but I did not perform for anyone but myself. I would stand before the long row of keys so that I was free to move swiftly from one end of the piano to the other. Then I would make the keys begin to talk.

First I would have the deep notes demand in a giant's rumbling voice, "Little girl, who are *youuu?*" One of the pedals was a great help in making his voice growl on and on. Then, moving my right hand up as far as it could go, I would make the treble keys into a little girl's quaver.

"Oh, a giant is coming!" Her voice would be shy and stuttering because she was so frightened.

The giant with the loud voice would begin tramping toward the small girl then. *Boom! Boom!* His steps thundered, particularly when I could get my right foot planted firmly on the loud pedal. Then I would make the sound of my heroine's feet scurrying to safety.

I had to do all this quickly, because before long, some adult would call in, "Jean, stop banging on those keys." At that point the story would have to change to one where everyone murmured. That was not nearly as much fun.

Once, when Grandma came in without my noticing, she shook her head at me and said, "We'll have to start your piano lessons soon. Pianos are for making music, not for making a racket."

I smiled at her and slipped away. I did not explain that I did not want to make music; I only wanted to tell stories.

Today, though, she wasn't trying to teach Hugh and me to play. She had a finger game to teach us. She did it for us first while we watched. I moved closer. She linked her hands and made her index fingers stand up tall. As she recited, her hands changed position somehow. I stared at them fixedly.

> Here is the church.
> Here is the steeple.
> Open the doors . . .
> And here are the people.

Three-year-old Hugh laughed with delight as Grandma flipped her hands over. Suddenly her fingers turned into a double row of worshippers.

"Let me," he cried. "Let me."

I edged closer to him and stared at his hands as step by step he copied her. She recited the words. Each time his fingers changed position, she gave a pleased nod. I pretended I was kindly letting my little brother go first.

"Jean, did you see how to do it?" Grandma asked.

"Yes," I muttered. Biting my bottom lip and keeping my eyes fixed on my own hands now, I began. I interlaced my fingers. I heard a small sound of protest from my grandmother, and Hugh drew in his breath. I hurried to get to the end and prove I didn't need either of them to correct me. I made the church doors with my thumbs side by side.

"Open the doors," I sing-songed. Then, turning my linked hands over, I said triumphantly, "And here are all the people!"

Only they weren't there. I stared in dismay at my two flat palms. The people were on the wrong side of my hands. It had not worked.

"I knew you had it wrong," Hugh crowed.

"Let me show you again, dear," Grandma said. "To start with, your hands must be like this."

I didn't look. Hugh thought he was so smart. I'd show him. If I just went slower, I could make it work.

"I know how. Watch," I shouted at them.

I began. As soon as he saw my hands form that church roof, Hugh yelled with laughter.

"Grandma, she's doing it wrong again!" he gurgled.

If Grandma had not caught hold of my right wrist, I would have dealt him a resounding slap. How dared he do it right the very first time?

"Watch me, child," Grandma commanded, ignoring Hugh. She repeated the finger play. I tried to see what I had done wrong, but it was impossible. Her fingers were all the same pinkish colour. Tears further blurred my vision.

My grandmother saw what was happening and let her hands fall to her lap. For a moment she was at a loss. Then she reached for my hands. She turned them back to back and began to coax each finger into the correct position.

As I realized my mistake, I pulled away from her, tears forgotten, and started over.

On the front porch of our house in Tai-pei. Standing are Aunt Gretta, Dad and Mother. Grandma is holding Pat, and Hugh, Jamie and I are sitting on the steps.

"Here is the church," she encouraged me.

"I'll say the words myself," I said, shooting a smug glance at Hugh. He might have done the actions perfectly right off the bat, but Grandma had had to recite the rhyme.

This time when I reached the last line, I had the congregation all present in two orderly rows.

"Well done, both of you," Grandma said. "Now I have a pretty new song to teach you."

She twirled the piano stool so that she faced the keys and played the tune for us. I liked it. Then she sang the words.

> "Come away," sang the river
> To the leaves on the tree.
> "Let me take you a journey
> That the world you may see."

I began trying to memorize the words the moment she started to sing. I wanted to be quicker than Hugh. I was relieved that this time there were no actions to follow.

"Let's try singing the first verse through," Grandma said.

She and I began to sing. But before we had reached the end of the verse, I no longer cared about proving how quick I was at learning. I was picturing instead the bright leaves fluttering down from the high branches. I had never seen leaves falling that way but I knew they did it in Canada, the faraway "home" the grown-ups told us of. Mother had told us of their glowing colours. Dad had explained that the season when they drifted down was crisp and cool. Canadians called it "fall" or "autumn."

They had four seasons in Canada. I knew all their names and what they were like. In Taiwan, the only season people talked about was the rainy season, when all that fell were millions of raindrops. I liked the sound of Canadian fall better.

This song was not just pretty. It told a story. I could feel how excited the leaves were, blowing down from the golden trees to the wide, shining river.

Then Grandma sang the second verse.

So the leaves, gently falling
From the tree to the shore,
Sailed away on the river
To return nevermore.

The final line pierced through my pleasant dream of Canada. My eyes stung with tears.

"Sing it with me," my grandmother said.

Hugh began to sing with her, but the lump in my throat stopped any sound from coming out.

"Jean, sing," Grandma told me.

She played the verse over again. Hugh sang. I stood mute and miserable. Grandma stopped playing and looked at me more closely.

"What's the matter now, child?" she demanded, her voice edged with impatience.

How could I explain that what was wrong was that when the river had invited the leaves to sail away and see the world, it had not told them that they could never come home again. I saw them, bright and beautiful, floating off on the surface of the water. They would have a lovely day. But then night would come. They would try to turn back. And the river would carry them on into the darkness, away from their tree.

If I told Mother, she would understand. But Grandma was not Mother. Grandma thought being afraid was funny. Grandma would tell the grown-ups about it at lunchtime and make a big joke out of it. She was laughing at me now.

"It's a pretty song," she said. "What on earth is wrong with you? Listen to your brother. He knows it already and he's two years younger than you are."

I blinked back my tears. Hugh was smiling. I straightened my shoulders, sent my brother a look of scorn and sang the song right through.

But I would always feel its sadness. To Grandma, it was only a pretty song. To me, it was a story.

I was only five that morning. I did not think about the power words had to loose my imagination. I did know, though, that I could go inside a story and live there, whether it was with Tom in *The Water Babies*, with the leaves longing to go home, or with the people I could bring to life when I made the piano keys talk to each other.

❧ 3 ❧

It was Sunday afternoon. Grandma had gone back to the Happy Mount Leprosarium where she lived with Aunt Gretta, who was the superintendent there. The house was filled with the peace that comes when company leaves.

Dad and the boys were outside shooting with bows and arrows. Mother was sitting in the big wicker chair, reading. She chuckled. Encouraged, I fetched my baby book and went to sit on her lap. She helped me up but went on reading.

I flipped back the blue-grey cover of the large album and stared in fascination at the first page.

Mother had started photograph albums for each of us, but mine, I thought, was the nicest. Hugh and Jamie's books just had pages covered with pictures, but my book had thin sheets of white paper between the thick black pages. The first few were covered with Mother's handwriting. They told about things I had done before I could remember.

Mother was still reading. I knew better than to interrupt. Interrupting someone who was reading was just as rude as interrupting two people who were talking. I heaved a loud sigh, though, to let her know I wanted her attention.

"Just let me finish this chapter," she said, her eyes still on the book. "I only have one page to go."

I sat quietly. But I craned my neck so I could make sure she did not cheat and start the next chapter.

She read the last sentence and set the book aside.

"Tell me what it says," I said, pointing to the first white page in my baby book.

"It says you weighed seven pounds, six ounces when you were born," she told me. "This was a bit of your hair when you were newborn and this was when you were six months old."

I stared at the two small tufts of hair. The first wisp was much darker than the second. Then I turned over a couple of pages, glimpsing snapshots of Jamie when he was three, myself as a baby and Mother and Dad before they were married. I found the page I wanted.

"Read this," I commanded.

Mother was silent. I looked up into her face. She was smiling a little and waiting.

"Please," I amended hastily. "Please, Mummy, would you read this page to me?"

She began at the top, although she knew which sentence I was waiting for. She had first read it to me after Marilyn had told me I had bad eyes. Ever since, I had loved going back over the questions I had asked that day and hearing, again and again, her answers. She had written the sentence shortly after my first birthday. She read it to me now.

You are a most impatient child!
But we love you and are so glad you can see.

I settled into the curve of her arm for the ritual.

"When I was born," I prompted, "I couldn't see, could I?"

"No. You couldn't."

"Why couldn't I?"

"Because you were born with scars on your corneas. The cornea is like a window in the front of the eye. It has to be clear if you are to see. Yours were all misted over. We could not see your pupils at all."

This was not my favourite part, but I did not rush her. I liked to listen to every detail in order.

"Then what happened."

"After awhile, we noticed that no matter how we laid you down in your crib, you were always facing the light when we came to pick you up. We moved your bed to a different place in the room, but you still turned toward the window. We began to believe you could tell light from darkness."

"Tell about the other baby."

"You know all this by heart," Mother protested, laughing. "You could tell *me* about that baby."

"No. I want you to tell it."

"When you were four months old, I was at the hospital examining a baby just your age. I put my stethoscope down beside him for one second and right away he reached out and tried to grab it. I realized then that you had never reached for anything. Not once."

"You were sad, weren't you?" I said.

She nodded.

"Then what?" I breathed. This was the best part.

"Then, one day when you were sitting at the little table your grandpa made, and I was feeding you your lunch, you suddenly reached out your hand for a spoon."

"What did you do?"

"I cried," she said. Her voice always grew husky as she told this bit. "But they were tears of pure joy."

I cuddled close to her and smiled. Now came the final funny part that made it all sound real.

"After you cried for joy, what did you do?"

She gave me another little squeeze and laughed. "I went on feeding you your lunch," she said. Then she started easing me off her lap.

I clutched the heavy album to my chest and looked forlorn.

"But who will read to me?" I asked.

Mother grinned. "Maybe it's time you learned to read to yourself."

"Will you teach me?" I dropped the photograph book and grabbed for her hand. "Can we start today?"

"Not today," she said. "But I will teach you."

"When?"

"Soon," she said. I sighed. At least that was better than "We'll see."

Even though I could not yet read them, I loved books passionately. One of the first words I ever said was "Book-a." I knew most of the fairytales by heart. I knew the Three Little Pigs, and the Three Bears. Why, I wondered, did things in stories always come in threes? You got three wishes. All the kings had three sons. Why didn't they ever have two boys and a girl like us?

I knew things *about* books, too. I knew the most important one was the Bible and the second most important was the dictionary. In Canada, they had places called libraries which were crammed with books. I had seen bookstores near our house in Taipei, of course, where the books were written in Chinese characters. Yet our books came not from libraries or bookstores, but by mail. Some were sent by aunts as presents. Some were ordered by my parents. Whenever a parcel of books arrived, it was like Christmas.

My favourite books came from England or

America. I knew about Christopher Robin and Alice going to Buckingham Palace. I knew about the Little Colonel going to the mansion where her grandfather roared at her. I knew about the curious little elephant going to "the great, grey-green, greasy Limpopo River all set about with fever trees." I did not yet know about Anne Shirley going to Green Gables.

All the adults in my family enjoyed reading aloud, although no two of them did it exactly alike. When Mother got caught up in a story, she skipped boring bits and read faster and faster. Grandma read every word, drawing out the exciting parts, dropping her voice to a thrilling whisper or bellowing with rage. My father, on the other hand, read straight ahead, without skipping or high drama, but showing his enjoyment of the words themselves by the delight in his voice. Whichever one read, I loved listening. The only trouble was, so much of the time they were too busy.

If I could read to myself, I would never have to wait for one of them to be free.

"Can I learn to read today?" I kept asking in the days that followed.

"Not today," my mother said. "But soon."

Then one morning when she called me, there was something about her voice that brought me on the run.

"I'm here," she said from the sewing room door.

My steps slowed. I didn't want to sew. Grandma had tried teaching me, but my stitches were always too big. The cloth got puckered. I kept pricking my finger like Snow White's mother.

But when Mother beckoned me into the room, I found everything changed. Gone was the lacquer chest full of little drawers filled with buttons. Gone was the sewing machine and the ragbag and the piles of mending. In their place stood a child's desk with a top that slanted up, so that whoever worked at it could see her book without having to hunch over. Near the desk stood an easel with great sheets of stiff, creamy paper propped up on it. The huge pages had writing on them. I ran to look more closely. I stared in delight at the large black words, printed in letters an inch tall. Bright pictures had been cut from magazines or traced from book illustrations and pasted next to the words.

I looked up at Mother. She smiled down at me.

"How would you like to learn to read?" she asked.

"Yes, please," I breathed.

"Now you know why you had to wait to begin," she said. "I had a lot to get ready. Your dad had the desk specially made. And we had to send to Canada for large print books."

I did not care about all this. I just wanted to begin. I pulled away and stared at the mysterious combinations of familiar letters.

"Stand up here in front of the easel," Mother told me. "You can walk up and down in front of it while you read the words. This word says CAT."

I stared at it. CAT. There was a picture of a cat next to it. Underneath it was DOG. I could tell by its picture. But I backed up. Next to the picture of the cat were two words, not just one. CAT cat.

"What's this one?" I asked. Then, before she could answer, I saw. They must both be words for "cat," one in big letters, one in small.

"That says cat, too, doesn't it?" I asked.

"Clever girl," said my mother.

This was going to be easy. I looked at the next picture and without any help at all read the words. "This says dog."

There was nothing to it. I whizzed down the rest of the page. I felt as though I had been reading for years. Then Mother flipped to the next page. The pictures were gone.

It was not going to be quite as simple as I had thought.

When I did eventually progress to reading an actual book, it was a lovely big one with cream-coloured pages and large, clear type. Even so, I had to put my face very close to the page to be able to see the shapes of the words, and my nose brushed against the paper as I tried to read. The book had a good smell. Not all books had that wonderful smell, I was to learn. Luckily, my very first reading book was a pleasure to my nose as well as my eyes and my mind.

My biggest problem was making the letters stay still while I looked at them. They often wavered and sometimes seemed to jump.

"If the b's and the d's would only stay still, it would be much easier," I told my mother.

Mother took my hand in hers.

"It isn't the letters that are moving," she explained. "It's your eyes. You have nystagmus. That means you have trouble keeping your eyes focussed on one spot for more than a second at a time."

"What did you say I had?" I asked, startled.

"You have nystagmus," she repeated. She spoke as though it were rather clever of me. Mother never said "doggie" when she meant "dog." Aunt Gretta did and so did Grandma. But my parents treated both words and children with respect.

When Jamie had turned nine, he had started going to the Canadian Academy, a boarding school in Kobe, Japan. The day I finished reading that first book with its boring stories about Muff, a dog, and Puff, a cat, I got Mother to write him a letter.

"Tell him I can read now. Tell him that I can read about Robin Hood just as well as he can. Say I can read fat books," I instructed.

Mother looked at me. I saw her mouth twitch.

"All right," I said before she could argue. "Write that I will be able to do it very soon."

Her pen began moving across the page. I smiled.

Little by little, reading became my greatest joy. I still had trouble keeping the letters from jiggling, especially when I was tired. And the books I read before I was seven were fat only because they were in enlarged print. But by the time I started going to school with other children, I knew I had been right when I had thought it would be wonderful to be able to read to myself. It was.

⚹ 4 ⚹

I could not go to sleep. It was too early. I could hear someone downstairs laughing, birds cheeping and all the busy street noises beyond the compound wall. I sat up, sighed and punched my pillow.

Laying my head down again, I gazed around my small room with satisfaction. In our house in the city of Shokwa, where we had lived when I was only four, I had had to share a room with Hugh. But now I had my own room. If I were in here with the door shut, anybody who wanted to come in had to knock first. Even Mother and Dad.

A small gust of wind fluttered my new curtains. In the half-light, I could not see them clearly, but I knew exactly how they looked. They were blue with white eggshells all over them. The shells were broken in half and out of each came a little white chicken. All the chicks were fluffy and their beaks and feet were a rosy red. I loved the curtains better than anything else in the room. Mother had made them especially for me.

I was not a bit tired! If I could get Mother to bring me a drink, she might sit on my bed and talk to me while I drank it. I knew she was getting dressed to go out for dinner, but it could not hurt to try.

"Mummy," I called, "I'm thirsty."

I waited. I thought she had not heard me. Then she came in dressed in her slip. I sat up to take the glass. But instead of handing me a drink of water, she seated herself on the edge of my bed and said something so astonishing that I forgot all about pretending to be thirsty.

"I have a surprise for you," she said, smiling down at me. "I think you'll be pleased. I'm going to have a baby."

I stared at her, open-mouthed.

"Well, think of that!" she said with a chuckle. "This is the first time I can remember you being struck speechless. Wouldn't you like a baby sister or brother?"

I gave a bounce in the bed. Joy filled me to the brim. "I'd like a sister," I told her. "I'm tired of being the only girl."

"I'll do my best," she said.

"When will she come?" I asked.

"Sometime in April."

"You mean, you don't *know*?" I was startled. Mother usually knew exactly when things were going to happen.

"It's up to Pat," she said, laughing again.

"Who's Pat?"

"The baby. We're going to call him Patrick if he's a boy and Patricia if she's a girl. Either way, this baby is going to be Pat. Now, do you think you could go to sleep?"

Sleep! How could I possibly be expected to go to sleep when I had this new person called Pat to think about? Mother got up, but before she could escape, I caught her hand.

"Where will she sleep?" I wanted to know.

"We'll see when the time comes," Mother said. "I really must finish dressing, honeybunch. Sweet dreams."

I lay there after she had gone and made up stories

about this little sister I was soon going to have. It would be like having a live doll. I could dress her and give her a bath. None of my dolls could be put in water. And I could take her for walks. By the time she was old enough to listen, I'd be able to read as well as the grown-ups. I'd read her the story about Eeyore's birthday. And I'd teach her "Come away, sang the river."

It was a long time until April. I almost forgot about the baby as the weeks passed. And when April did arrive, Pat did not. Grandma and Aunt Gretta came instead.

When we woke up on Easter Sunday morning, though, Mother, Dad and Aunt Gretta were nowhere to be seen. Grandma hustled us into our clothes and, to our amazement, took Hugh and me over to the Dicksons' before breakfast. Such a thing had never happened before. Mrs. Dickson seated us at the table with Ronnie and Marilyn and then went back out into the front hall with Grandma. We could hear them whispering out there. The four of us strained our ears, but it didn't do any good. We stared at each other full of uneasiness.

"It must be something to do with Easter," Marilyn said finally. When Mrs. Dickson came in, she asked her right out. "Is there going to be an Easter surprise?"

Mrs. Dickson gave a snort of laughter. Then she looked around at our bewildered faces. "I suppose you could call it that," she said and laughed again.

"When will we see it?" Marilyn's eyes sparkled.

"It's not for us," her mother said quickly. "It's only for the Littles. I don't know when. Now, Hugh, how about some fruit to start with."

After breakfast, we went into the living room and

sat in a circle while Mrs. Dickson read the Easter story
to us. I did not really listen. I stared at Mrs. Dickson's
face instead. Whatever the secret was, she knew all
about it. And she was having a hard time paying
attention to the story herself. She kept looking up
from the page. She was watching the window.

"Go quickly and tell his disciples that he is risen
from the dead," Marilyn's mother read out.

Now I was watching the window, too. That was
why I saw Grandma first. Only her head showed
above the sill, but she was *running*. Mrs. Dickson shut
the Bible with a bang. I stood up and waited for
whatever was coming.

Grandma rushed right into the Dicksons' house
without stopping even to call a greeting. She was out
of breath from running, but her beaming smile eased
the tight knot of nameless anxiety in my stomach. I
thought she was going to burst out with some wonderful news like the women in the Easter story.

But she just looked at Hugh and me and, still
beaming, said, "Go home, children. Your daddy
wants you."

We did not wait to ask one question. We dashed
out of there, sped across the wide lawn and flew in
through our own front door.

Dad was there in the hall waiting for us. He was
beaming, too.

"Who do you think is upstairs?" he asked.

We stared at him.

"Mummy?" Hugh tried.

"Who else?" Dad asked, his smile even broader.

I felt as though I were about to fly apart into a
million pieces.

"Aunt Gretta?" I said.

"Someone much smaller than Aunt Gretta," Dad said.

Then we knew.

"Pat!" we shouted and ran for the stairs.

As we went slam-banging up them, we heard a cranky wail. It sounded as if our new sister or brother did not like being here. It also sounded astonishingly alive and real. Not a bit doll-like.

We reached the door and there she was, wrapped up in a yellow and white towel, bellowing. Her face was scarlet with what looked like rage, and her fists beat the air. Gulping, I stepped forward and held out my arms to take my sister.

Aunt Gretta would not give her to me.

"She's brand new," she told us over the racket Pat was making. "I have to bathe and dress her. Then she'll want to sleep. You can hold her later, Jeanie."

I backed up, relieved but resentful, too. Hadn't they been promising she would be a live doll for me to play with? Now Aunt Gretta was keeping all the fun to herself. And why was the baby so cross and so noisy? Couldn't Aunt Gretta make her hush?

"Can she see me?" Hugh asked, waving his hand in front of her puckered-up face.

"Not really," Aunt Gretta said. "But her eyes are fine."

I heard the relief in her voice. Had they thought she might have bad eyes? I suddenly was not sure I even liked her.

I did want to love her, though. She opened one of her baby fists. Even opened wide, her hand looked so tiny that I had trouble believing in it. A little fearfully, I stretched out my right index finger and softly touched her palm. Instantly her hand clamped shut, gripping my finger. When I tried to pull away gently, she hung on for dear life.

She liked me! I smiled shyly at her. Having a baby sister was going to be pure joy.

"She's a Sunday's child, isn't she?" Hugh said.

I turned my head and scowled at him. I knew what he meant. He was thinking about one of the rhymes Grandma had taught us.

> Monday's child is fair of face.
> Tuesday's child is full of grace.
> Wednesday's child is full of woe.
> Thursday's child has far to go.
> Friday's child is loving and giving.
> Saturday's child must work for a living.
> But the child who is born on the Sabbath Day
> Is bonny and blithe and good and gay.

Jamie, and now Pat, too, were Sabbath Day children. Hugh had been born on a Friday. But I had come into this world at three o'clock on a Saturday afternoon.

Mother had tried to tell me it was a fine thing to work for a living, but she could not fool me. I saw right away that the best day was Sunday and the second best was Friday. Saturday, along with Wednesday, were the worst. I pulled my finger out of my baby sister's grasp. She should have had tact enough to be born on a Wednesday.

"Sunday's child she is," Aunt Gretta said, laying the baby against her shoulder and patting her back. "Not only Sunday but Easter Sunday! She's an extra-special girl."

She crooned the words and rested her cheek

against the baby's downy head.

I was not so sure. I felt that anyone who started life by being born on Easter Sunday was definitely a show-off.

"I want to see Mummy," I said loudly. Dad came with us. Mother was in bed. I had never seen her in bed in the daytime. She looked tired. Then she smiled at us and the world stopped being a strange uncomfortable place. I sighed with relief.

"What do you think of your new sister?" she asked. I forgot about being Saturday's child.

"She's awfully little," I said.

"No. She's not awfully little. She's Pat Little," my father said.

Hugh and I laughed uproariously at this clever joke. Mother closed her eyes and groaned.

"Don't you get it?" Hugh said. "It's funny."

"I get it," Mother said. "It's just that I've heard it before."

As I went back downstairs, I puzzled over this. How could she have heard it before? After all, Pat had just been born that morning.

At first Pat slept most of the time. She had a basket near Mother and Dad's bed. But before long, the day came when she had to have a room of her own.

"You and Hugh can go back to sharing a room for awhile," Mother told me. She was changing Pat's diaper. She did not look at me as she spoke. "If she's in here, I'll be able to hear her when she cries at night."

I gazed at my blue curtains with the baby chicks. I so loved lying in bed looking at them. Having them there made night less frightening. I remembered watching Mother hang them. Had she meant them for Pat all along? Being a big sister was not pure joy, after all. You had to be unselfish. You had to share.

I hated sharing.

But perhaps Mother did not yet know what a bad sister I was. If I pretended to be happy about letting that baby have my room and my blue curtains with the chicks, she might go on believing I was "loving and giving."

I stifled a great sigh before my mother could hear it.

"It's all right," I lied bravely. "I don't mind."

Mother turned and looked at me. The smile in her eyes told me she had seen right through me. The tenderness I saw there said she knew me even better than I did and loved me still.

"Good girl," she said softly.

⚹ 5 ⚹

Hugh and I were in the back seat of the taxi. Crammed in with us were bags holding the things we would be using during our trip from Taiwan to Hong Kong. I felt squashed and tired of waiting.

But I was excited, too. We had not seen Grandma or Aunt Gretta or Dad for weeks. My grandmother and aunt had gone home to Canada. But Dad had only gone to Hong Kong. He would be waiting on the dock to hug us and take us to our new house. In just one more day we would see him.

Pat was ten months old and I had turned seven when we left Tai-pei that day. Dad had agreed to fill in as superintendent of the Matilda Hospital while another doctor took a year's leave. After that, Mother said, we might be moving to Japan while Dad did much the same thing in Kobe.

I liked the new house in Hong Kong, on the Peak. The furniture all belonged to somebody else so we couldn't bounce on the beds or kick the chair legs. But on clear days we could see way out over the blue ocean, and on dull days our house was so high up the mountain that it was actually in the clouds.

When we were settled, Mother and Dad took me by ferry across the narrow strip of water that separates Hong Kong from China to visit an eye specialist in the city of Kowloon. I had been to other eye doctors, but I had been so young then that I could not remember those visits. I held on tightly to my parents' hands.

The doctor sat me in a black leather chair with arms. Then he went to stand by a chart on the far wall. He told me to put my hand over my left eye. Then he pointed at the big capital E at the top.

"What is this letter?" he asked me.

"E," I said confidently.

He moved his hand down to a line of much smaller letters.

"What do you see in the next line down?" he wanted to know.

I peered at the distant chart. Could that first one be a C? Or was it a D? I turned my head a little to the right and looked at it over my nose. That sometimes seemed to steady things. I squinched up my forehead. Nothing helped.

"They're too small to read," I muttered. "If I went closer . . ."

"Never mind," he said, as if he thought I did not know the alphabet. He did not let me go nearer. "Now cover your right eye," he ordered. "What do you see?"

I did my best to find that E again, but with only my left eye, I could barely make out the pale oblong of cardboard. The big E had faded into a faint smudge.

"I can't see any of them," I admitted. I felt as if I had failed a test a baby of five would have been able to pass. The doctor shook his head and tut-tutted with his tongue. He turned away from the chart.

"20/200ths visual acuity in the right eye," he said to my parents, "but only 12/400ths in the left. Dear me."

I stole a glance at Mother and Dad. Their faces were serious. Then Mother reached over and gave my hand a comforting squeeze.

"Well, this is much better news than we hoped for

when she was born," she said. "It is wonderful that she sees as well as she does."

Then Dr. Ling turned my chair a little and pulled a strange apparatus toward me. While I rested my chin on a ledge, he shone a painfully bright beam of light into my eyes, first the right and then the left. He spoke from behind the light.

"Look at me," he said. I tried. But the piercing light was so strong that my eye flinched and slid away. It also began to water.

"Keep your eye still," the doctor said. "Try to hold it still."

I wanted to go home. The tears were real now.

"I've never seen eyes like hers before," he said as he gave up at last and let me rest.

Finally, Dr. Ling had me look at the chart through various lenses. Then the doctor said such a wonderful thing that I forgave him for making my eyes ache. He could give me glasses that would help me to see better.

We could not get my spectacles that day. I thought they would never come but finally they did. I had two pairs.

Trying on my new glasses (*I smirked at the camera.*)

"These are for seeing things at a distance," Dad told me, "and these are to use when you read."

I tried both pairs. I could not tell them apart. I felt stupid. I did not tell my parents that whether I looked through the distance glasses or the reading glasses, everything appeared the same.

Dad took pictures of me wearing them. I smirked at the camera. After all, both Mother and Dad wore glasses. Glasses were a grown-up thing. No child I knew had them.

The next day, Mother was out most of the morning. When she came home for lunch, she was smiling.

"The principal at the Peak School says they will be glad to have you two," she told Hugh and me. "You are both to start when the new term begins in April."

"What kind of school is it," Hugh demanded suspiciously.

"It is a small school. They have just twenty-five students in a class, mostly the children of foreign business people," Mother told us.

I was not sure how I felt about facing a class full of strange children until I saw the uniform worn by the girls. It consisted of sleeveless cotton dresses in pastel pink, green, blue or yellow. Each dress was trimmed with white rick-rack braid. And every dress had matching underpants. I had never had underwear resembling a rainbow before. It was elegant. If you turned a somersault and your pants showed, you could be proud because that proved you were a Peak School girl.

I could hardly wait to begin.

❦ 6 ❦

"This is Jean Little," my new teacher told the class. She led me to a desk.

"This is Pamela, Jean," she said, smiling at the girl in the desk next to mine. I smiled at her, too.

Pamela's cheeks got pink. She looked away. I thought I knew what was wrong. She was shy. I sat down and waited for lessons to start. I was glad that reading was first.

When it was my turn to read out loud, I held the book up to my nose as usual. The other children giggled. The teacher hushed them. Then she turned to me.

"Are those your reading glasses?" she asked.

I was not sure. I snatched the glasses off and switched. But I still had to hold my book so close that my nose brushed against the page. Everybody stared. Nobody noticed my good reading.

That afternoon when the teacher left the room, Monica pointed at me.

"Look!" she crowed. "She's got black all over her nose!"

I clapped my hand to my face. The class burst into peals of laughter. They only broke off when the child nearest the door hissed, "Shh! She's coming."

When the teacher walked into the room, I longed to tell, but I didn't. I knew tattletales were despised by everyone. I spat on the corner of my handkerchief and scrubbed my short nose until it felt raw. But a red nose was better than a nose smudged with printer's ink.

The next morning nobody sat with me at break. That afternoon, Jane waved her hand before my face.

"How many fingers am I holding up?"

"Three," I said.

She *had* been holding up three. But the minute I spoke, she popped up one more and pushed her hand within an inch of my nose.

"*Wrong!*" she jeered and hooted with laughter.

"That's mean, Jane," Pamela said. She marched over and gave me half of her orange. When I smiled at her, though, she backed away. She had a kind heart, but she did not want to be turned into an outsider, too.

I was shocked and bewildered by their scorn. Even when Marilyn had told me that I had bad eyes, she had not laughed about it. Taiwanese children had occasionally made fun of us because of our light skin, but they had not seen any difference between me and the other foreign children. Nobody had made me feel I looked peculiar when I held things up close. Nobody until now.

I was gradually learning that if you were different, nothing good about you mattered. And I had not really understood, until now, that I was different.

"You are going to have riding lessons," Mother told us one day.

I was delighted. Most of my classmates went to Kowloon to ride horseback. Maybe I'd be so good at riding that the others would want to be friends with me after all.

But real horses were not like the horses in books. They were enormously tall and they tossed their heads and stamped their great hooves. They also rolled their eyes and blew down their noses in an alarming manner. Their teeth were awesome. I had to be coaxed before I dared go close enough to pat a long, bony nose. As I jumped back, the horse curled his rubbery lip at me, and the other children laughed. Hugh and I were given ponies to ride that first day. They were smaller, much to my relief. They had carried many children on their backs and they were resigned to it. Slowly we jogged around and around the pony ring.

A man shouted orders at us. "Keep your hands down. Rise with the horse. Grip with your knees. Backs straight. *Rise!*"

He told us to watch the others, but I could not see what they did with their hands or their backs. My fat knees were incapable of gripping. I jounced up and down. What did he mean by "rise"? My bottom hurt. I wanted to go home.

The second week, Hugh, who was only five, moved up to the horse ring. I stayed on my small, shambling pony. I felt relieved but humiliated. I was now the only child left going around and around the pony ring. I struggled not to cry.

I gave up hope of being a star rider.

"You are going to start gymnastic lessons," Mother announced a few weeks later. She sighed as she said it. Hong Kong, with its British emphasis on class distinctions, was not an easy place to raise children. If she wanted us to have friends, we had to do what the other English-speaking children were doing. But its effect on us was beginning to worry her. She had come into my room one morning and found me lying back while our Amah, who took care of us while our parents worked, put on my shoes. Mother had soon put a stop to that. Yet all the foreign children went to gymnastic classes. They were given by one of the British wives. I was different enough already, she knew. So she had arranged for us to join the others.

I did not know what gymnastics meant, exactly. This time I was less hopeful. I remembered the pony ring.

We did the gymnastics on somebody's lawn. We began with somersaults. I was slower than most of the others. I puffed and panted more. But I could do them. I knew, at once, that I would never shine here, either. Yet as I managed those somersaults, I hoped that I might blend in.

"Now we're going to turn cartwheels," said the teacher in a jolly, encouraging voice.

She showed us how. I stared, concentrating all my attention on her agile body, but no matter how hard I tried, something dire happened when I attempted to make my feet spin through the air. I always toppled over sideways and ended up in a heap. I got redder and redder and I ran out of breath.

At first I was not the only one with problems. Yet, given time, one after another succeeded. And as they landed neatly on their feet, they would glance at me and seemed to smile in a superior way.

"Try, dear. Try, try, try again!" sang the lady.

I flopped over ten times more. Then I got fed up with trying. I went home in tears. I hated gymnastics.

A week later I received an invitation to Marguerite's seventh birthday party. The only parties I had been to before were family ones. This was a proper party. The whole class was invited. My invitation came in the mail. Our mothers came, too. I wore my prettiest dress and my strap shoes.

First, there was a magician. I could not see the tricks, but I clapped when everyone else did. Then we went outside to play games. Our mothers sat in a group nearby and watched. I could tell where mine was by her blue dress. They began with Pin the Tail on the Donkey. I did just fine. My tail was a lot closer to that donkey's rump than most of the others.

"Now we're going to play Drop the Handkerchief," the lady in charge called. "Everybody get in a circle."

We sat in a ring on the grass. I had not played this game before, but I decided it would be easy to copy the others.

"Marguerite can be It first," said the lady, "since it's her birthday."

Then they all began to sing.

I wrote a letter to my love
But on the way I dropped it.
A little doggie picked it up
and put it in his pocket.
I won't catch you . . .
And I won't catch you . . .
And I won't catch you . . .
But I WILL catch you!

As the children chanted this, Marguerite skipped around behind our backs with a handkerchief in her hand. She touched the top of my head and skipped on by. This was easy. All I had to do was sit and sing this song. I was good at songs.

Suddenly, over on the far side of the circle, where I

couldn't see, there was a shriek and people went dashing around. Before I could figure it out, somebody else was skipping past, singing. I tried to see her face as she came near. It was Nancy . . . or Jane. I turned my head to see her go the rest of the way around.

Then, right behind me, a voice screeched, "But I *will* catch *you!*"

"Run, Jean! Run!" They were all yelling at me.

"It's behind you, stupid," the girl next to me shouted. "Grab it and *run!*"

I twisted around. There was the handkerchief on the grass right behind me. I jumped up and reached for it. Where had Jane gone? I must be supposed to chase her. But I couldn't see her. And they were all screaming with laughter.

I started off after her.

"Not that way! Silly idiot! The *other way!*" shrieked my classmates. They were beside themselves with glee.

I turned and ran to the one person I knew understood and loved me. Mother! I flung myself into her lap, my eyes filled with hot, shameful tears.

Later, when we talked about it at home, I learned that my mother had no idea that I did not know what was happening, that I could not see across to the other side of the circle. Later I found out that other mothers had talked to her about overprotecting me, and she was trying to show them she did not do so.

But at that moment, all I knew was that she was not hugging me close and comforting me. Instead her two hands turned me around to face the mob of tormentors.

"Jean, you have to be a good sport," she said. "Go

back and play with the others."

I stumbled back. I was pushed in the right direction. The rest began to chant again. I clutched the handkerchief. I wanted to mop my tears away with it, but I knew that would not be the right thing to do.

"I won't catch you . . ." they began singing.

I kept on going, still bewildered.

"She's not going to drop it," Marguerite's voice shrilled. Another gale of laughter interrupted the song.

The lady in charge bent over me.

"And I *will* catch you," she carolled.

She pulled the handkerchief from my fingers, dropped it behind Jennifer, took my hand and ran me around the circle. Jennifer knew better than to beat the lady to the empty place. The lady and I reached it and she plunked me down.

"Go on, Jennifer, dear," she called. "But don't pick Jean."

I was too miserable to be grateful. I sat there, hunched up, not looking at any of them. As the game went on and nobody paid any attention to me, I grew calm enough to fish my own hankie out of the pocket of my dress. I wiped away my tears. I did not blow my nose, although it needed it. I feared the sound would set them off again. I waited for the game, the party and the day to be over.

Mother had betrayed me. That was, by far, the worst thing that had happened.

We trooped inside and watched Marguerite blow out her seven candles. I stuffed cake into my mouth. My cheeks got very hot. When Elizabeth spilled her lemonade all over her party dress, I laughed as loudly as anybody. Even though I still did not know the rules for Drop the Handkerchief, I had learned how little girls behaved at proper parties. When Elizabeth jumped to her feet, stared down at her ruined dress and began to sob noisily, I poked the girl next to me and we both bent double, choking with mirth.

Deep inside, I hoped Mother was not looking. But mostly I felt heady with triumph. For once, I was not the one who was different.

⚔ 7 ⚔

Hugh and I were hurrying up the hill that led to the hospital grounds and our house. We were eager to get there because our big brother Jamie had come home from boarding school for his summer holidays. His classes were over a week before ours.

"Wait for me," I called to Hugh, who was far ahead.

A car stopped beside me. A man called through the open window, "You're Llew Little's kids, aren't you?"

I nodded. Hugh came running back.

"I'm going up to see your dad. Would you like a lift?"

"Yes, thank you," we chorused. We scrambled into the back seat. The car purred up the hill to our gate. We jumped out, calling back our thanks. We swaggered a bit when we saw our ten-year-old brother watching.

"Who was that?" Jamie asked as the car moved off.

"I don't know. He's a friend of Daddy's," I shrugged. "I'm the best reader in my class."

"You mean you took a ride with a stranger?" Jamie sounded shocked.

Hugh and I looked at each other. Why shouldn't we accept a ride from one of our father's friends?

"He's a friend . . ." Hugh repeated.

"That man might have been a kidnapper," our big brother told us in an ominous voice.

We moved closer. His next words were spine-chilling.

"Kidnappers steal children. Some sneak up and grab you when you're out alone. Others offer you a ride. They gag you so you can't scream for help. Then they take you down into a dark cellar and they tie you to a chair. Very tightly! Then they write to your parents asking for money. They say, IF YOU DON'T PAY US THE RANSOM, WE'LL KILL HER."

I gasped. *Her!* He was talking about me.

"Then what happens?" I breathed.

"You're making it up," Hugh said. He ran off. I stayed right where I was. Jamie's eyes bored into mine.

"If your parents send the money, the kidnappers just ask for more. If your parents say they haven't any money, the kidnappers come down and saw off your hand. Your right one."

This was so gruesome I could hardly bear it. But it fascinated me at the same time.

"Your mother goes to get the mail," my older brother said, "and there is a package. When she picks it up, she finds that it is *bleeding!*"

I gave a small moan. Poor Mother.

"When she opens it, she sees her little girl's hand. She faints dead away at the terrible sight," Jamie said.

When I had gashed my leg on a nail while I was climbing a fence, Mother had been perfectly calm. The ladies having tea with her had looked shaken, but she had just taken me to the bathroom, cleaned the cut and bandaged it. I opened my mouth to tell Jamie and then closed it again. If my whole hand were sawn off and she could not get to me with peroxide and bandages, even Mother might swoon.

Jamie, seeing that he had lost my full attention for a moment, talked louder and a bit faster.

"When she regains consciousness, she tries to find the money. If she can't get enough to pay the ransom, another bleeding parcel arrives."

"My other hand?" I whispered.

Jamie was tired of hands.

"Your right foot," he told me solemnly.

He went on to explain that after your hands and feet were gone, the kidnappers proceeded to chop off your ears. At last you died from loss of blood. In agony, of course.

He was getting bored. He gave a last word of warning.

"That man in the car probably let you go free because he saw me watching and knew I'd be able to identify him. *Never* get into a car with a stranger."

He turned to walk away.

"Mummy wouldn't let . . ." I began to bleat.

My big brother stopped in his tracks. He turned on me.

"You mustn't say a word to her about it," he said. "She would be terrified," he added hastily, before my suspicion had time to take root. "You don't want to scare your own mother to death, do you? Promise you won't say a word to her about it."

"All right," I said unwillingly.

I wouldn't tell her. From now on, I would just be on the watch for strangers — especially sinister men carrying gags or saws. If one of these offered me a lift or started sneaking up behind me, I'd run. I'd run like the wind.

By that June, Japan and China had been at war for over a year. Dad, reading newspaper accounts of the advance of the Japanese army, wanted Mother to take us to Canada. He thought war was coming and we would be safer out of Hong Kong. He could not come because his job would not end for six months. But he thought we should go. Mother did not want to.

School ended. My teacher came to talk with my parents about my education. She said I needed more individual attention than she could give me. She advised them to enrol me in a Sight Saving class in Canada.

When she left, Dad turned to Mother.

"That settles it. I'll get your tickets tomorrow," he said.

We sailed away from Hong Kong on the *Empress of Canada* bound for Yokohama. It was hard to understand why we had to leave Dad behind. But saying goodbye to him was helped by Hugh's kicking his sandal overboard just as the ship was leaving the harbour. I watched with horrified fascination as it flew toward the water and was swallowed up.

In Yokohama we boarded the Japanese ocean liner *Hiye Maru* for the journey across the Pacific to Vancouver. I stared around, awed and excited by the noise and bustle of the crowd. Having lived in Tai-pei and Hong Kong, I was used to throngs of people. But there was something different in the mood of these travellers pressed close to the rail.

We children had wormed our way to the very front. I peered down the ship's steep side. The slice of green water between us and the dock widened. Then long streamers of bright coloured paper looped through the air. People on the dock caught them and unwound them. They stretched across the gap, glowing ribbons joining us to the world we were leaving. All around us strangers were crying, waving, calling

"Goodbye" or "Sayonara." I stared up at Mother and then at all the other adult faces wet with tears, yet smiling. Were they happy or sad?

My brothers were waving as though they knew someone on the dock. I strained my eyes, but I could not make out any individual faces. Not to be outdone, I waved, too.

One-year-old Pat, in Mother's arms, chortled with excitement.

"Ohh," the crowd breathed, as though all those pressing against the rail were one person giving a huge sigh. It took me a moment to realize why they had all sighed at once that way. Then I saw. The streamers had begun to break. One by one they parted, the torn ends fluttering down into the oily green, reaching waves.

The ship's horn blew a large, sad noise that made me jump. I looked up at the other passengers. Some were Japanese or Chinese, some foreigners like us. As the horn sounded once more, tears pricked my eyes, too.

The gap grew really wide. We were on our way.

As we made our way down to our cabin, I heard a woman say to a man in a uniform, "Purser, there haven't been any submarines sighted, have there? There's no chance we'll be torpedoed?"

Mother was making her way through the crowd, still carrying Pat and with Hugh clutching a fold of her skirt. Jamie and I followed. I thought about what I'd heard. Wasn't a torpedo something dangerous? I turned to my big brother.

"What's a torpedo?" I asked.

He glanced at me. I'd seen that look on his face before. I could not quite remember when. He smiled.

"I'll tell you later," he promised, "when we're alone."

℥ 8 ℥

Uncle Harvey, Mother's older brother, was at Union Station to meet us when our train from Vancouver chugged into Toronto. We were grubby and exhausted after having spent several days and nights in a crowded compartment. Both Hugh and I hung back a little, not recognizing the tall man who bent down to kiss our small mother.

We went to the apartment where Grandma and Aunt Gretta were living. We had no trouble remembering them. There were hugs and kisses all around and a babble of talk.

The next afternoon, Grandma and Aunt Gretta came with us to visit Aunt Eva and Aunt Ruth. We got hugged and kissed again. Jamie, Hugh and I tried to look as though we liked it. We knew that these sisters of Dad's had presents waiting for us.

Aunt Ruth had written while we were in Taiwan to tell me she had won a beautiful doll in an office pool. She was to be mine, but I would have to wait until I came to Canada to get her because she might break in the mail.

Aunt Eva gave Jamie and Hugh an impressive box of Tinker Toys first. We had never seen things like them. The boys dumped them out on the carpet and began building. I stayed sandwiched between Grandma and Mother on the couch, my eyes never leaving Aunt Ruth's face.

She pretended not to know why I was gazing at her so intently. She smiled at Mother over my head.

"Gorrie, we've been counting the days. It's so wonderful having you all home again," she said, settling into an easy chair. Aunt Eva had a softer heart.

"Ruth, don't be mean," she said. "Jeanie wants her doll."

Aunt Ruth burst out laughing. As she heaved herself out of the chair and went toward the bedroom, she reached out and rumpled up my hair. I pulled away. I didn't know these new aunts, but even though Aunt Ruth was the one who was about to give me a doll, I already liked Aunt Eva better.

"Here she is!" Aunt Ruth cried, reappearing with the loveliest doll I had ever beheld. "Do you like her?"

She beamed at my obvious delight. She knew what a prize this doll was, and she was proud of having won her for me.

Years later she told me that when she had been a small girl, her widowed mother had been too poor to buy her a doll. Aunt Ruth had played with three kitchen chairs instead, giving them names, dressing them up in remnants of material from their rag bag, and making them hold long conversations.

But at this moment, I hardly knew Aunt Ruth was there. My whole attention was given to the doll in her arms.

She was a baby doll in a filmy pink dress. She had a smile just for me. And she was almost as big as Pat.

I reached for her, forgetting all about saying thank you. But Aunt Ruth did not let me take her.

"Wait a minute," she said. "I have something to show you first. Look here."

She sat down again, turned my new doll over on her side and showed everybody her right leg. I peered at it, puzzled. The boys stopped playing to watch. Hugh's head was level with the doll's chubby leg. His eyes widened.

"There's writing on her," he said in a startled voice.

"Yes. Can you read it?"

Hugh could not read. I scowled. I wanted my doll and they were wasting time. Jamie pushed Hugh to one side.

"Allan Dafoe," he read out.

Everybody but me looked at Aunt Ruth. None of us children knew who Allan Dafoe was. I reached for my doll again, and this time my aunt let me have her. Over my head, she told the story of how she had got the autograph.

"The day I won her, I was walking along the hall at work carrying her," she said, "when Dr. Dafoe came out of the board of health office and saw me. I knew who he was because his picture is in the paper so much. He asked me who the doll was for. I said I was giving her to my seven-year-old niece who was coming home from Taiwan. Then I saw his pen sticking out of his pocket, so I asked him to autograph her leg. He said he'd be happy to, especially for a little girl coming such a long way."

"Who is he?" Jamie asked.

"He's the doctor who delivered those darling Dionne quintuplets." Aunt Ruth told him. "You'd know his name if you'd been living here. They just turned five years old. Imagine having five little sisters all the same age. They're only a few months older than Hughie."

Both Jamie and I shuddered at the thought, but Aunt Ruth did not notice. Hugh wanted to know what a quintuplet was. Aunt Ruth told him all about Cecile,

Annette, Marie, Yvonne and Emilie. She even had pictures of them.

I marched out of the room so I would not have to listen to any more talk about those silly girls. I didn't care how famous this doctor was. I hated having his name scrawled in blue ink on my baby's leg. It was insulting.

I hugged her close to me. Her head, arms and legs were made of bisque, but her body was stuffed. As I squeezed her, she cried "Ma'ma!" Her voice was like a lamb's bleat, but I loved it. Between her lips, which were parted slightly, I could glimpse two small white teeth.

I carried her into the bathroom where I could be alone with her. I sat on the toilet seat and examined her all over. Her hands were fat and dimpled, with the fingers curved realistically. Her grey eyes closed with a small click the moment I laid her flat. Her eyelashes were real. She had white socks and shoes with straps across the tops. She also wore a bonnet, a petticoat and underpants. She didn't have real hair. Her head had been moulded to show where her hair was. It was light, like mine. She was perfect.

Except for that man's name on her leg.

"Susan," I murmured to her. "I'll name you Susan."

The grown-ups gossiped. Hugh and Jamie sat on the rug making something unrecognizable with their Tinker Toys. I could see them through the door, which I had left slightly ajar.

The doorbell rang. More people! I was sick and tired of being kissed. I stayed where I was. Maybe they would not miss me.

No such luck.

"Jean," Aunt Ruth called, "there are some people here who want to see your new doll."

As I came in, Aunt Ruth reached out and drew me over to her.

She introduced me. Then, taking Susan, she hurried on to tell of meeting Dr. Allan Dafoe. As she reached the climax of her story, she turned Susan upside down to display the name on her leg. She started to point out the autograph and then stared at the spot where the signature had been moments ago.

There was a long silence. I could feel my face going red and hardening into what Grandma called my stubborn expression. I stared at the floor.

"Where's Dr. Dafoe's name?" Aunt Ruth demanded.

I raised my chin and glared at her.

"I washed it off."

"Why?" Aunt Ruth asked, bewildered and beginning to be angry. "That signature would be worth money in a few years. What ever possessed you . . .!"

"Babies don't have names on their legs," I told her, grabbing Susan back into my own arms where she would be safe.

Again there was a moment of startled silence. Then all the adults were laughing. They thought it was funny.

"Isn't that darling?" one of the strangers cried.

I was outraged. I shot a glance at my mother. She was not laughing at me. She would never have let somebody write on Pat's leg, either.

Vastly comforted, I turned my back on the rest of them and stalked off to the bathroom again. This time I locked the door. I sat down and straightened out Susan's dress, which Aunt Ruth had rumpled.

"Canadians are silly," I muttered. I went on using words I'd heard Dad use. "They are asinine. Idiotic."

Then I lowered my voice to a whisper and used the worst insult I knew. "Canadians are jackasses!" I told Susan.

Susan smiled.

Pat and Susan in Toronto
(*My beautiful doll was almost as big as my sister.*)

On Sunday morning we went to the biggest church I had ever been in. Mother and Dad had been married there by the minister, Dr. Pidgeon. When we arrived, we stopped to leave Pat in the nursery. I was surprised. In Taiwan babies went to church along with everyone else.

A man led us to a pew near the front. Grandma and Aunt Gretta went in first. Mother motioned for Hugh to go next, but he hung back, trying to make me go in before he did. Jamie turned his head away and pretended he was not with us as we scuffled. Mother detached Hugh and, going first, led him by the hand so he sat beside her. She motioned Jamie to sit between us to keep the peace. Feeling ashamed, I edged in last.

Copying Mother, I bowed my head and prayed silently, "Help me to be a good girl."

Then I raised my head and sat absolutely still, trying to behave like an angel who'd just flown in straight from Heaven. I stole glances at Mother. Was she noticing? She was. She sent me an approving smile over the heads of my brothers. I relaxed very slightly, folded my gloved hands on my lap, swung my feet gently and prepared to enjoy myself.

Church, I had discovered, was a good place for thinking about things. Also, when the sermon started, Mother would produce from her purse prescription pads and stubs of pencils so we could draw pictures. Grandma had humbugs in her purse, but I liked the paper and pencils better.

The service began. The organ made a far grander noise than the one in Taiwan. I sang the children's hymn lustily when it came, even though it was one that always worried me.

> God sees the little sparrow fall.
> It meets His tender view.
> If God so loves the little birds,
> I know He loves me too.

I still could not see how God's merely "seeing" the small sparrows falling proved He loved them. If He really cared, wouldn't He reach out and catch them somehow? I had asked about this, but nobody had had a satisfactory explanation. I sang anyway. After all, there were a lot of things about God that were puzzling. I trusted everything to be crystal clear as soon as I was bigger.

Then Dr. Pidgeon began to pray. I bowed my head and stopped swinging my patent leather shoes. When he said, "Let us now pray in the words that Jesus taught us," I was ready.

The next instant I was shocked. Dr. Pidgeon was saying the familiar words, all right, but instead of joining in and helping him, these people were mumbling so softly you could hardly hear them.

I jerked up my head for an instant and stared around at all the bowed heads. How mean these Canadians were! They were making Dr. Pidgeon do it all by himself. That was not the way to pray. I knew because I had been to church lots of times in Taiwan. You were supposed to say the words in a clear, loud voice. As if you meant them!

I myself would show that poor man up there that he was not alone. I, for one, would join in properly.

"Thy kingdom come," I bellowed, setting the entire congregation of mumblers a good example. "Thy will be done on earth as it is in heaven."

Jamie tried to shush me. I went right on. If Jamie wanted to sit there mute, let him. I was not so unfeeling.

Dr. Pidgeon and I led the entire congregation of Bloor Street United Church in prayer.

"Forever and ever, *Amen!*" I finished proudly. I had kept up with him all the way to the end. Mother must be pleased.

On the way out, we stopped to shake his hand. I was proud because he smiled at my mother like an old friend. She introduced us. She left me till last.

"And this is Jean," she said, an odd quiver in her voice.

Dr. Pidgeon put his hand gently on my head. We smiled at each other. He was grateful to me, I could tell.

"Yes," he said gently, his voice quivering also. "I noticed Jean."

✖ 9 ✖

Before school began, Mother took me to Dr. Lowry, the Canadian eye specialist who had examined my eyes during the brief furlough our family had spent in Canada when I was three. He gazed at my two pairs of glasses. Then he got me to put the distance ones on and look at a chart that was exactly like the one in Hong Kong. Now I had to look at it first with the glasses on and then without them. Either way, I could still only see that same old big E.

"Humph," he grunted. "Those aren't any use to her, and I'm quite certain that the reading glasses aren't helping, either."

I stared as he tossed them into his big wastebasket.

"You'll have to take her to Aylesworth," he went on. "Those Sight Saving classes are his baby. He decides whether children have too little or too much vision to be admitted. He may think she should go to the School for the Blind. Tell him you've brought her all the way from Taiwan to get her into a Sight Saving class. That should do the trick."

He was right. Dr. Aylesworth wanted to persuade parents to put their visually impaired children into special classes. Telling them that two Canadian doctors had brought their daughter halfway around the world to enroll her helped.

We moved into a house on Kingswood Road in Toronto. There was a Sight Saving class at the nearby Duke of Connaught School. Aunt Gretta and Grandma moved in with us.

On the Sunday before school opened, World War II began. To me it seemed exciting, frightening and totally unreal.

I had learned so much with Mother that I went right into grade two. My teacher, Miss Burton, was kind. And everybody in my class had bad eyes.

Our classroom was special. The chalk was fat and yellow instead of skinny and white. The blackboards were *green*. No other room in the Duke of Connaught School had green blackboards then. The enormous dictionary, which lay open on a stand, had large black print. Each desk had its chair attached to it and all of them could easily be moved so you could sit as close to the board as you needed to. The desk lids, which we used for writing and reading, could be tilted up and down like the one I had had in Taiwan.

When Miss Burton printed on the board, she did it in large letters. The thickness of the chalk made her lines fat and much easier to see than ordinary chalk marks. Most of the children could read them from their desks. Even I could often puzzle them out.

The others could all see better than I could. This was true despite the fact that I was the only child in the class who did not have to wear glasses.

"Why do glasses help them and not me?" I asked Mother.

Mother drew me a picture of the inside of the eye. The cornea was at the front. My corneas were scarred. Glasses could not take away the scars. Behind the cornea was the iris. My iris was stuck to my cornea in places. Behind the iris came the lens. Glasses could fix things that were wrong with the lens. My lens seemed to be fine.

"Oh," I said, not really sure I understood.

"It is as though you put on fogged-up glasses first and then put other glasses on top. Because of the foggy ones, the glasses in front would not do you any good, would they?"

"Can't they fix it with an operation?"

"No," Mother said. I learned that a corneal transplant or graft was only appropriate when the rest of the eye was undamaged. Even when this operation became common, it was not suitable for my problems.

Knowing I could not take in too much at once, Mother did not explain then that my pupils were also eccentric or "off centre." This meant that they could not fuse the images they got into a single picture. Instead of seeing one world through two eyes, I saw two slightly different worlds and looked at them through one eye at a time. While I looked through my right eye, my left slid in toward my nose. When I switched over to the left, the right slid over in the same way. This was called strabismus. I learned later that the expression commonly used was "cross-eyed."

Because I saw only a small area at a time, I had never observed, while looking in the mirror, that my eyes crossed. By the time I got close enough to see my eyes clearly, my nose was touching the glass and I could not see past it to the eye I was not using.

Even though I had less vision than the others, I loved Miss Burton's class. Everybody held books up close. There were several different grades in the one room, since there were not enough children with poor eyesight to fill a class otherwise. Outside its walls, we might feel different, but once we walked through our classroom door, we knew we belonged.

Every day Jamie and I left our house on Kingswood Road together. We walked as far as Queen Street side by side. When we got on the streetcar, though, he sat with his friends, and I sat by myself. I knew exactly when to get off because all the children on the street-car scrambled off in a big bunch. At noon and after four o'clock, I followed my big brother to the streetcar and I sat near him. I got off when he did. It was simple.

Then one day Jamie had to stay home. I was not worried. I went to the stop, proud that I knew my way. When the streetcar came clanking up, I hopped on it, feeling like a world traveller. At the school stop, all the children got up and herded toward the door as usual, I among them.

I did not worry about the trip home, either, until I had been on the streetcar for several minutes. It was not until then that I realized I needed Jamie. I peered through the grimy window at Queen Street. I saw cross streets and dim buildings blur past. They all looked unfamiliar.

The driver called out the names of some stops. I listened hard. But he said the names so fast. How many had I already missed?

I looked around for help. Why weren't the grown-ups in the seats nearby asking me who I was, where I was going, and why I was out alone? In Taiwan and in Hong Kong they would have. Did Chinese people care more about children than Canadians did? If only I could see better, I might find a friendly Chinese face right here.

"Look at that kid, Ralph. She's cross-eyed."

The boy who had spoken was sitting right in front of me. He was a big boy, bigger than Jamie even. He was with another boy about the same age. I saw the other boy's head jerk around. The two of them were staring straight at me.

"Cross-eyed, cross-eyed!" the second boy sing-songed, his voice low but ugly.

Bewildered, I stared at them. Seeing that I did not understand, they both burst into raucous laughter. "Look at her. She's so dumb she doesn't even know her eyes are in crooked. Hey, cross-eyed kid, go home and look at yourself in the mirror."

"Boy, I wouldn't *ever* look at myself, not if I had eyes like hers. I might scare myself to death. Come on, buddy. This is our stop. So long, Cross-eyed."

They got off the car, jostling each other in the aisle.

I sat staring after them as the streetcar clanged away up the street. What had they meant? My eyes were not in crooked.

I knew, however, that I could not see people's eyes as clearly as the rest of the family. They talked about us all having blue eyes like Dad's except for Pat. Pat's were hazel like Mother's. I could not see what colour anyone's eyes were unless I was nose to nose with a person. Could I also have missed the fact that mine were crooked?

The driver called out another street name that I could not hear. I remembered that I was lost. Should I get out, even if it were not the right stop?

I shivered as I thought of standing alone on a strange street corner, having no idea where I was. Besides, we always stayed on the streetcar for a long time, didn't we? Maybe all I had to do was wait a little longer. Or ask somebody.

Once more I began to search the faces around me, trying to find a friendly grown-up. The streetcar was only half full, but even so there were lots of other passengers. Yet none of them seemed to notice me.

A big man in a raincoat sat down next to me with a thud. He filled up two-thirds of the seat. I stole glances at his face as he opened a newspaper and started to read. He looked grumpy.

I needed help so badly, though, that I would have to take a chance. If I did not ask him, I would have to squeeze out past his big knees. They touched the seat in front of us. I swallowed and planned what to say. Then I turned.

KIDNAPPER SOUGHT

The words leapt out at me. I stopped breathing. Kidnappers! There really were kidnappers. Until that moment, I had believed, deep down, that Jamie had invented them simply to terrorize me. He hadn't. I thought of the bleeding parcels and I stared at the powerful hands turning the pages of the newspaper.

I did not say a word.

More people got on the streetcar. Some chatted to each other but most rode along in morose silence. Almost everybody looked like a kidnapper. I stared out the window and quaked.

After what seemed like years, the man beside me folded up his paper, jammed it under his arm and, without once glancing at me, got off. I did not move even though he was no longer in my way. I was worn out with worrying and watching. I just sat and waited for my ordeal to end.

It started to rain. The lights inside the streetcar made it look as though night was falling. I could see my face now, dimly reflected in the grimy glass. I looked like a ghost. The car jolted and swayed along, stopping at every corner. Now there were fewer people. Finally the very last woman pushed through the doors and disappeared. Only the driver and I were left.

He turned and stared back down the long empty car at me. Tears started rolling down my cheeks.

"Little girl," he asked, "where are you going?"

"Kingswood Road," I sobbed.

"Well, you haven't got far to go then," he said cheerfully. "That's just three stops back. Didn't you hear me call it?"

I could not explain about my bad eyes or the man who might have been a kidnapper. I shook my head. I could not find a handkerchief in my sweater pocket. I rubbed away my tears with its sleeve. More came spilling out. I made my way to the door a stop ahead of time.

"Not this one," the driver called back.

I waited wordlessly.

"Kingswood Road," he called at last.

I stepped down onto the chancy step which made the doors open, but which snapped up again the moment your weight was off it. Usually streetcar steps made me a little anxious. Tonight I did not even pause to place my foot squarely in the middle. I just scrambled awkwardly down to the wet curb.

When I actually arrived at our house, dusk had fallen. I stumbled up the short walk. I used both hands to turn our front doorknob.

Before I could get all the way into the house, Mother was there, snatching me up into her arms.

"You're safe," she cried. "Oh, Jean, what happened? Where have you been?"

Holding on to her for dear life, my face pressed into her shoulder, I sobbed out my story. It was muddled. I forgot to mention the kidnapper. As I clung to her, gulping out a confused explanation, Mother finally understood that I had gone to the end of the line because I had not been able to recognize the corner of our street. She said very little, just held me close for a long, long moment. Then she set me on my feet and spoke in her usual brisk voice.

"Why don't you go and put your pyjamas on right now? You look as though you are fast asleep on your feet. But some supper will help. I'll call you when it's time."

I did not ask her about kidnappers or crossed eyes. I went up and got undressed. When she came to call me, I had fallen asleep.

When I wakened an hour later, Mother brought my supper up and served it to me on a low table that went across my knees. Using it made me feel special, as if I were really ill. Mother tucked another pillow behind my back and handed me my napkin.

"Read to me while I eat," I said, knowing that she was feeling extra fond of me. I also needed a story to come between me and the difficult things that had happened.

"All right," she said. "But wait till I get the others. I have a book I've been wanting to read to you, but I want you all to hear it."

I did not protest. Even though I would have liked to have her attention all to myself, I knew I was ahead of my brothers already, what with having my supper served to me in bed. I could be generous this once. I wanted them to see me, anyway, sitting up against my pillows like a queen.

The boys came, Hugh in his pyjamas and looking sleepy, Jamie trying to look as though he were almost too grown up to be read to. Mother opened the book and began.

> When Mary Lennox was sent to Misselthwaite Manor to live with her uncle, everybody said she was the most disagreeable looking child ever seen. It was true, too.

I laid down my spoon. From the first sentence, *The Secret Garden* seemed especially mine. I did not wonder what Mary Lennox looked like. I knew. She looked exactly like me.

Mary had clearly not been born on a Sunday, either. She, too, was selfish and bad-tempered and lazy. She even tried to get Martha to put her shoes on for her. I wasn't the only one who had done such a reprehensible thing.

Yet little by little, she grew into somebody quite different. And the way it happened made perfect sense. I knew that I, too, would be different if I could find a hidden garden and friends like Dickon and Colin and the robin.

I had made two journeys that day, one to the end of the streetcar line and one to Misselthwaite Manor. I never cared to ride to the end of the line again, but over and over I would return to that vast and mysterious house. And always, when I got to the long walk, Mary herself would be waiting to take me through the door to the secret garden.

☻ 10 ☻

We had only lived in the house on Kingswood Road for a couple of months, when the man who had rented it to us decided to move back into it himself. My family found a new house on Bedford Road. It was already furnished. A portrait of the owner's father hung in our dining room. He looked stern, and no matter where you stood in that room, his gaze seemed to follow you.

I no longer had to go to school on a streetcar. Jesse Ketchum School had a Sight Saving class and was so close that we could easily walk there and back. My new teacher's name was Miss Bogart, and I learned to love her before my first day in her class ended. There were students in the class through all the other grades up to grade seven. There were only two of us in grade two.

When the bell rang for morning recess that first day we all put on our coats and went outside. I went home, thinking that it was noon already.

When I walked in the door of our house, Mother gave me a startled look, glanced quickly at her watch and said, "What are you doing home at this hour?"

"School was over," I protested faintly. "Everybody went home. They put on their coats. I saw them."

"They went out for recess, honeybunch," Mother said. "It's all right. I'll write you a note."

"I can't go back. They'll laugh. I might get the strap."

Mother knew Miss Bogart would do no such thing.

Ignoring my wail, she sat down and wrote a note for me to take to my teacher.

"Couldn't you come with me and explain?" I asked.

Mother shook her head. "You can do it yourself," she said firmly, as if she had enormous faith in me. "Just give her the note and she'll understand."

I hurried, hoping to get back before the bell. But the playground was empty. I steeled myself to go inside. If only this had not been my first day! They would be bound to laugh. It would be like the Peak School all over again.

I opened the heavy door and tiptoed through the deserted halls. The door to my classroom was open. Miss Bogart was standing there watching for me. I blushed scarlet and handed her my mother's letter.

She took my hand and led me to my desk. All the others had their heads bent over their books. Nobody stared. Nobody laughed.

My teacher drew up a chair and sat down beside me. Then she opened the note. When she looked at me, she was smiling.

"When I was six," she told me, "I did exactly the same thing, Jean. My mother was so surprised to see me."

"So was mine," I admitted. When she laughed gently, I was able to laugh, too. The next thing I knew, I was telling her about Susan. The doll had become my constant companion at home. I had other dolls who were merely dolls, but Susan was my best friend.

"I wish you'd bring her to school," said Miss Bogart. "We'd all love to see her."

When I looked around at the others, they had stopped pretending not to have noticed. They were all smiling at me, even the girls in grade seven. When I went back that afternoon, I took Susan with me. With my doll sitting beside me, I felt at home in Miss Bogart's room. The other children in the class had been together for over two months before I joined them. After I had been with them for a week, I left Susan at home. I didn't need her any longer.

Because of Mother's teaching, I was ahead in my schoolwork. Miss Bogart did not mind my going to listen in to the lessons given to the other grades, as long as my own work was finished. I learned about the explorers that year. And I read not only my own reader, but the reader for grade three. One poem in it began:

My child, should you decide to go
And make your home in Mexico,
The proper place for you to settle
Is on Mt. Popocatepetl.

I liked the name of that faraway mountain. In an idle moment, I taught myself to spell this interesting word, first forwards and then backwards. When I did it for Miss Bogart, her eyes sparkled behind their glasses. After that, whenever some grown-ups came to visit the Sight Saving class, Miss Bogart would get me to spell Popocatepetl backwards for them.

Inside that room, I was happy all day long. Miss Bogart gave me a notebook and had me copy a poem on the first page.

Good, Better, Best!
Never let it rest
Till the Good is Better

And the Better, Best.

I gazed at the words, so neatly printed. I said them over, enjoying the way they sounded. It was the first time I had written out a bit of "poetry" and seen its shape.

When that first notebook was filled, there was a new rhyme to be written on the opening page of the next notebook.

When a string is in a knot,
Patience will untie it,
Patience will do many things.
Did you ever try it?

This time even though I printed the poem just as carefully, I was not nearly as pleased with the result. The last two lines were so flat and tame. They lacked the wonderful tongue-rolling swing of the lines "Till the Good is Better / And the Better Best."

Also it was not true. No matter how patient I was, I hardly ever could untie a knot.

Jesse Ketchum was a rough and tumble place outside the safety of Miss Bogart's class. One day I was allowed to take Mother's best umbrella to school as a special privilege. A big boy in grade eight snatched it from me before I could get it inside the school, upended it and stamped his big foot on each of the spines, breaking it beyond repair. When I entered my classroom, I was in a flood of tears and the umbrella was trailing limply behind me like a dead bird. Nothing could be done to fix it. And I could not see well enough to be able to identify the boy who had broken it.

As I wept, Miss Bogart began to hear stories from the other children in the class. At first they were all about how we had been teased and tormented in the schoolyard. But soon other sorrows were spilling out. Everyone, even the oldest boys and girls, felt useless compared to other children. We couldn't thread needles. We couldn't knit. We couldn't deliver papers because we couldn't see house numbers. We couldn't make change quickly. We were called Four Eyes, everybody except me.

"Cross-eyed! That's what they yell at me," I said.

"If only we could do something clever, better than other kids . . ."

Miss Bogart listened to our wistful voices, to our anger and our hurt, to our feelings about ourselves. She did not say much. But we saw an expression on her face, a look of purpose. She was going to come up with an idea.

When she told us a day or so later that we were going to weave wastepaper baskets, nobody felt comforted. We knew we'd be no good at it.

When she brought the things we needed, we still did not believe it was going to be wonderful. All those long skinny white reeds did not inspire confidence. They looked like nothing on earth.

Yet as my wastepaper basket grew, I was dazzled. It wasn't a silly pretend craft, designed to be thrown together in half an hour by inept children. It was something a grown-up could be proud of having made.

We did not do it all in one day. We worked slowly, painstakingly. When we finally completed them, Miss Bogart told us to print our initials on the bottom so that we would know which basket was ours. They were all going to be painted at the School for the Blind. She did not explain why. Nobody asked. The baskets were taken away.

Then, just before Christmas, the baskets were delivered back to Jesse Ketchum. I stared at the beautiful dark-green baskets in astonishment. None of them looked like mine. Had they lost it?

Miss Bogart turned one over and read out the initials. It wasn't mine. I watched one of the girls reach out eager hands for it.

"F. J. L." Miss Bogart read.

I jumped. Flora Jean Little was my full name, even though I was always called Jean. I stood up and stepped forward. She smiled at the doubt and wonder in my expression. She turned the beautiful basket upside down and the two of us stared together at the tall, crooked initials I myself had pencilled there.

"Is it yours?" my teacher asked gently.

"Yes," I said in a small, husky voice.

Hugging it to my chest, I carried it back to my desk.

Dad came from Hong Kong to spend Christmas with us before he went on to the job he had promised to do in Japan. We got up at five in the morning to go and meet his train at Union Station. I was secretly afraid I might not recognize him, but I knew him the moment I saw that rolling gait. We crowded close to him to be hugged. Pat, not understanding the great occasion, had fallen sound asleep while we waited. When Dad took her from Mother, she opened her eyes, gave him a doubtful look, and then flung her arms around his neck.

"Daddy!" she cried joyfully.

We exchanged smug looks. We had kept showing her his picture and telling her he was coming. Our efforts had not been in vain.

On Christmas morning, I gave my shining green wastebasket to my parents. They were as amazed as I had been. Jamie and Hugh stared at it. I felt puffed up with pride. For the first time I had done something really well. I knew that even Jamie could not have made a more perfect basket. Dad said that he himself couldn't have done it half so well.

I basked in the warmth of his approval. I did not feel cross-eyed all day long.

Dad came home to stay the following fall. He and Mother decided to go to live in Guelph, where he had lived as a boy. We moved in November. I was eight.

When the question of my schooling came up, Dr. Aylesworth examined my eyes again and decided that my vision was really so limited that I should go to the School for the Blind in Brantford. Miss Bogart disagreed. She told my parents and Dr. Aylesworth that she was sure I could handle a regular grade four class.

"If she goes to Brantford, she'll soon think of herself as a blind child," she said. "If she attends a regular class, she'll grow up thinking of herself as sighted and fitting into the sighted world and, after all, that is the world she'll have to live in when the years of schooling are over."

She was persuasive. Dr. Aylesworth recommended that I be enrolled in a regular grade four.

There was a blizzard the day we moved. The boys had gone ahead with Dad. Even so, the car was crowded, with me wedged in with last-minute luggage in the back, and Grandma, Pat and Mother in the front. The roads were slippery and darkness had fallen by the time we reached Guelph. The driving snow made it so hard to see that Mother drove by the new house twice before she recognized it. But when at last I followed her up the walk between the twin stone gateposts and stared up at the big stone house that was to be our new home, I forgot all about the long drive. The house was not as big as Misselthwaite Manor, but it looked like a storybook house all the same. All five large windows were lighted from within. The big cream-coloured double doors with their two brass knockers looked as though you would find adventures waiting on the other side.

In this new house, anything might happen.

I followed Mother through the girls' door of St. John's School. It was nine o'clock and the hall was empty. I stared at all the coats hanging on hooks outside the grade four classroom door. There were so many of them! I swallowed and hung back.

Mother, feeling my hand tug at hers, turned and saw the panic in my eyes. She smiled at me and paused long enough to murmur words meant to be comforting.

"Your teacher's name is Mr. Johnston. He knows we're coming. I'm sure you'll like him."

What she did not seem to understand was that it was not the thought of Mr. Johnston that was frightening me. I had no doubt that my teacher and I would like each other. I had not yet met a teacher who had not liked me.

The sound of children's voices came from behind the closed door. It was those children who worried me. How would they feel about a cross-eyed girl joining their class at the end of November?

Mother knocked once, opened the door and propelled me gently but inexorably into the classroom. The buzz of conversation stopped instantly. I knew, without turning my head, that every child in the room was staring at me. Out of the corner of my eye I glimpsed what seemed like hundreds of boys and girls seated in long straight rows. I later learned that there were only forty-one students in Mr. Johnston's room. But compared to the twelve students in Miss

Bogart's class, forty-one seemed like a multitude.

Mr. Johnston came to meet us, smiling a welcome. "You must be Jean," he said, speaking directly to me. "We have a place ready and waiting for you. Boys and girls, this is Jean Little, the newest member of our class."

There was silence. As he escorted me to an empty desk in the front row, our footsteps seemed to make a deafening clatter on the wooden floor. I slid into the seat, my head down, my cheeks flaming.

"See you at noon, Jean," Mother said, her tone casual.

I held onto the word "noon" the way a drowning man would clutch at a rope. Noon was only three hours away.

The teacher and my mother walked together to just outside the classroom door and stood talking in voices too low for anyone inside the room to hear.

From across the aisle, I heard a sharp whisper.

"She's cross-eyed."

I did not look to see who had said it. I was struggling to control the tears that were threatening to well up and spill over. Even though this was my first day in a regular classroom in Canada, I knew that crying right then would be a fatal mistake. I did not dare blink. I gazed straight ahead.

Mr. Johnston came back and the whispers stopped. He smiled down at me. The warmth of that smile dried up the betraying tears. I smiled tremulously back.

I did not know yet that being Teacher's Pet was almost worse than being a cross-eyed crybaby.

"Jean will have lots of interesting things to share with us," Mr. Johnston told the class. "She was born in Formosa. Who knows where Formosa is?"

Nobody knew. Nobody liked not knowing. The teacher went to the board, reached up and somehow released a map of the world so that it unrolled and hung down over the blackboard. He got a pointer and indicated the faraway island that the Chinese called Taiwan, where I had lived for the first six years of my life. As he did so, I saw that there was something wrong with his left arm and hand. He held it awkwardly and did everything with his right hand.

My new teacher was handicapped like me. But there was no time to think about this now.

"Here it is," he said, "right off the coast of China. Jean has also lived in Hong Kong."

His pointer moved to another invisible speck.

"Can you speak Chinese?" he asked me.

I was feeling happier. I nodded proudly. It did not cross my mind that with this introduction, Mr. Johnston was giving the bullies in the class added ammunition.

"Could you say Hello?" he asked.

I hesitated. When Christians greeted each other in Taiwan, they used the word for Peace. I knew that non-Christians used a different salutation. I decided to use the word my family used. These Canadians would not know the difference.

"Peng-an," I said.

A muffled titter sounded all around me. Too late, I realized that I should have kept quiet. Mr. Johnston frowned at the noise and the class hushed. I heard him sigh. He would keep trying to help. But nobody, least of all the teacher, could make them like me.

"Well, we are very glad you have joined us, Jean," he said to me. Looking at the others, he added, "I know you will all do your best to make Jean feel welcome here in Guelph."

I stood up with the rest to sing God Save the King and mumbled the Lord's Prayer. When I slid out of the desk, however, the hinged seat flipped up. I had never sat at that kind of desk before. It took me a second to find out how to make it drop down again. In my hurry, I let it go down with a resounding bang. There were more muffled giggles.

When the teacher gave me my reader, I opened it eagerly. I had to hold it up close, as usual, to see the words. I had no idea how odd I looked when I read, since I had never seen myself doing it. My nose touched the page, as always, and I moved both the book and my head back and forth as I followed the line of print along. I caught more smothered laughter, but I was too pleased with the new book to pay attention.

As the others took turns reading aloud, I realized with relief that I read as well as any of them, better than most. It was my turn. I would show them.

"Good, Jean. You read with expression," Mr. Johnston said as I came to the end of the page.

I glowed.

Then it was time for the writing lesson. Printing was easier for a visually impaired child to read than cursive writing which was taught in grade four. Because of this, I was not supposed to learn to write with all the letters joined together, but to go on printing. When Mr. Johnston's class got out the lined notebooks in which they practised rows of loops and squiggles, I had to be given a different activity.

That morning Mr. Johnston should have had me do extra arithmetic problems. Since I had skipped grade three, I was extremely shaky when it came to knowing my times tables. But Mr. Johnston gave me a box of coloured chalk instead and sent me to the board to draw a picture.

I loved doing it, of course. I drew a huge castle with a flag flying from its tallest tower. I put in trees. I felt I drew trees especially well. I used all the colours in the box. I did not feel the hostile glances aimed at my back. I was having fun while they worked.

No wonder, before the first recess bell had rung, I had forty enemies.

They never knew that I practised "real writing" like theirs at home and envied them their chance to use those specially lined writing books.

When we went out for recess, nobody spoke to me. It was as though I had suddenly become invisible. Everyone else knew what to do, where to go. I stayed close to the door, shivering in the November wind and wishing recess would end.

At noon, Hugh told us all about some boys he had met. I listened to stories about Dick and Bill Weber with a pang. Never mind. Perhaps I would make a friend that afternoon.

But nobody except Mr. Johnston spoke to me when I got back to school. We had a spelling bee. I was one of the best spellers in the class. I was slowest at arithmetic, though, and I could not see where the Eskimos lived on the big map. When four o'clock came, I was very glad it was time to go home.

The name-calling began the instant I left the shelter of the playground. Boys going in my direction started up the chant as soon as they knew Mr. Johnston could not see or hear them.

"Cross-eyed! Cross-eyed!"

"Chinky-chinky Chinaman!"
"Teacher's Pet!"

"Knock, knock.
Who goes there?
Little Jean Little
In her underwear!"

I began to run, but they swarmed after me, screaming taunts. I ran faster, my heart thudding, my eyes
blurring with tears.

"Crybaby, cry! Crybaby, cry!
Stick your finger in your eye
And tell your mother it wasn't I.
Crybaby, cry!"

As I fled, each pounding step jarred my whole
body. What would they do to me if they caught me?
Home was only five short blocks away, but even
though I positively flew along the sidewalk, it seemed
to take hours to get there.

In my breathless dash, I slipped on a patch of ice
and went crashing down on one knee. There were
shrieks of delight. They sounded so menacing that I
did not take time to inspect my wounds but was up
and running on like a fox with a pack of hounds after
it.

I had not realized before how fast I could run. I also
had not realized before how much I had depended on
my two brothers for protection when we lived in
Toronto. St. John's was a two-room school, with only
third- and fourth-grade classes. Hugh, in grade one,
and Jamie, in grade six, went to Victory School,

several blocks away. No longer were the boys there to help fight my battles. No longer could I threaten bullies with what my big brother would do to them. Sobbing with relief, I reached our house at last. The cat calls died away as I pulled open the big front door and stumbled inside. Then I stood still and wailed, "Mother!"

She came running and gathered me into her arms. "What happened?" she demanded, holding me close.

I displayed my torn stocking and scraped knee. She led me into the office examining room. Gently she peeled off my stocking and cleaned up the smear of blood.

As she tended my hurt knee, Mother listened to the story of the bullies chasing me home and calling me names. She did not gasp or shudder. Her calm helped to quiet my storm of tears.

"I want you to walk there with me," I finished up. "They'd leave me alone if you were there."

She did not answer at once. When she had helped me change into other stockings, she sat down in the rocking chair and took me on her lap. I was a bit big, but neither of us noticed.

"I'm so sorry you had such a bad time," she said. As she rocked the chair slowly back and forth, her cheek rested against my hair. Little by little, peace filled me. In drowsy content I listened as she went on, "But you'll have to learn to laugh at teasing, Jean. If I walked you to school each day, you would never make friends. Remember that rhyme . . ."

I remembered it. I did not like it. It was not true. I gave a wriggle of protest but she repeated it anyway.

"Sticks and stones

May break my bones,
But names will never hurt me."

"But names *do* hurt me!" I growled. "And I want
you to walk with me. I don't want them for friends. I
hate them."

"It is hard not to hate people when they've made
you so miserable," she agreed. "But you'll just have to
laugh it off. They won't tease you when they see that
you don't mind."

"But I *do* mind!"

She laughed softly, gave me a last hug and tipped
me back onto my own two feet. Didn't she care? I
knew the answer. Her calm, steady words did not fool
me. She hated anyone being cruel. She loved me very
much. If she could fix things, she would.

But this was something even my mother could not
fix. I would have to work it out for myself.

And I didn't know how.

Then why wouldn't she come and tell the teacher?
Why wouldn't she fight my battles for me?

Because they were my battles. Because she could
not win them for me any more than Mr. Johnston had
helped when he had told the others to make me
welcome.

The doorbell rang.

"Maybe it's for you," Mother said. "Run and answer it."

She was trying to distract me, I knew, but I went.

Mary Weber stood on the step and smiled at me. She lived across the street, and she was almost as old as Jamie. I waited politely to see who she wanted to see.

"Hi, Jean," she said. "Your mum says you like to read. I wondered if you'd like to come to the library with me and get some books?"

I stared at her blankly for a long moment. Then I totally forgot the name-calling and my sore knee.

"I'd love to," I said. "I'll tell Mother."

As we walked side by side down the snowy sidewalk, I felt too shy to start a conversation with such a big girl. I hoped somebody from my class would see us. If they found out Mary Weber was my friend, it might make a difference.

"Starting school in a new town can be pretty rough at first," Mary said gently.

I shot a startled look up at her. Did she know or was she guessing? She knew. Living right across the street, she travelled the same route as I did. She must have seen me fleeing from those boys.

"Yes," I said, comforted.

We went on in a friendly silence. Then she took my arm and steered me to the right.

"We're here," she said. "The Children's Library is

downstairs. The door is at the back."

Once we were inside, we went down a flight of stairs and entered a large room filled with books. Shelves ran around three walls and there were extra bookcases in front of them. In the centre of the room were some low tables with big picture books spread out on them. Windows at ground level let the last light of afternoon pour in. Right inside the door was a corner walled off by an L-shaped counter. Behind it, a woman was repairing books. Another lady stood at the long desk checking out books for a couple of boys. When they left, she smiled at Mary.

"Miss Metcalf, this is Jean Little," Mary said to her. "She wants to join the library."

"How old are you, dear?" the lady asked.

"Nearly nine."

"Can you write your name?"

I felt indignant. Of course I knew how to write my name! Then I realized she might mean "write" with the letters all joined together the way the others were learning to do at school. I thought fast. There were several letters I did not know how to make yet — z and k and y and a small j. But none of those were in my name. "Jean" was easy, but "Little" was trickier with that capital L. I tried picturing it. It went up and around in a loop, swept down and looped again in the opposite direction, didn't it? I could do it.

I nodded.

I had hesitated a little too long. Miss Metcalf studied me. I nodded again, emphatically this time.

"Come over here," she said.

She led us over to a smaller table with a huge book on it. Beside it was a big ink bottle and a straight pen, the kind you had to keep dipping. I had never used one of those before. It was not till grade five that you had an inkwell in your desk and learned to use a straight pen. Mr. Johnston's class were doing their writing lessons with a pencil. I had written with my parents' fountain pens, though. I knew you had to be careful not to press down on it. You weren't supposed to grip the pen too tightly, either. It was complicated.

Breathing hard and biting my tongue in order to concentrate, I picked up the long pen, dipped the nib into the ink bottle and began to write.

I had not known enough to let the excess ink drain back into the ink bottle. The first thing I did, on that tidy page, was make a black blot. The librarian tut-tutted. My face burned. I stared down at the stain. It looked gigantic.

"Never mind, dear," Miss Metcalf said in a kindly but faintly disapproving voice. "Go ahead."

My hand shook. I wrote "Jean" and paused for breath. Then I did the "L" carefully. I started at the bottom and drew it rather than wrote it, but when it was done, it looked all right. I sighed with relief and finished signing the register without any further mishaps.

My name was in the book.

A few minutes later, Miss Metcalf handed me my first library card. I took it reverently.

"You can take out four books a day," she rhymed off. "Two white card books and two blue. Or, if you like, four blue. Never more than two white cards in one day, though. You must take good care of them. If you keep them out longer than two weeks, there's a fine of two cents per book per day. Remember to be quiet, because other children are reading."

I liked the way she made reading sound important.

I understood, from the way the librarian spoke, that the library was a place sacred to books and the people who read them. Readers mattered here.

And I was a reader.

I followed Mary to the nearest set of shelves. They had the Ws on them. I ran my glance over the backs of the books. They did not have bright paper covers. Most of them had been rebound in dark wine or brown or blue. Their names, and the names of the people who had written them, were printed in gold on the spines.

Jean Webster, Kate Douglas Wiggin, Nelia Gardner White, T. H. White. I stared at them greedily. So many!

"Which are white card ones?" I whispered to Mary. It sounded mysterious, a secret language only taught to children possessing library cards.

Mary explained, also in a whisper, what the difference was. White cards were in the back of story books. *Heidi, The Secret Garden,* all the Oz books and the Anne books had white cards. The non-fiction ones, filled with facts every child should know, had blue cards tucked into the cardboard pocket inside the back cover.

I had not heard of the Oz books or the Anne books. But I knew right away that white card books were what I wanted.

Mary did not think to tell me that books of poetry also had blue cards in the back, and so did biographies. There really were some good books in the shelves of non-fiction. In time, I found them.

I wandered up and down, staring at the hundreds of books I could choose from. Mary went off to get books for herself. I took volumes down and flipped through the pages, looking for books with lots of conversation in them. With my impaired vision, it was easier for me to read short paragraphs than long, solid ones. I also liked books with people in them, and people tended to talk.

I left clutching *The Dutch Twins* and *Anne of Green Gables*.

From that day on, when I was chased home from school, I went straight to my library book. The moment I opened it, I stopped being "cross-eyed" Jean Little and instead became Rebecca of Sunnybrook Farm or Lord Fauntleroy. I wept over books, too, but those were healing tears. When I suffered with Emily Starr or Hans Brinker, I felt comforted. I and the book children I loved were all part of a great fellowship. I was not alone any longer.

The name calling did not stop. I did my best to laugh off the teasing, to ignore it, to believe that names could never hurt me, but I was not a brave child. I was a coward and, what was worse, a crybaby. I knew that if I could manage to look as though I did not care, my tormenters would find another victim. But I could not manage to appear other than terrified and humiliated. I always cried, however hard I tried not to, and I always ran.

At suppertime, when Dad would ask us to tell about our day at school, I began inventing incidents in which I was the heroine. When my lies grew too outrageous, one of the adults would tell us the story of the boy who cried wolf. We all grew heartily sick of that wretched boy.

One evening in January, I became desperate enough for attention to borrow a scene from a book called *Glengarry Schooldays*, which Mr. Johnston had been reading aloud to us.

"Because today was Friday," I began, "we had speeches and songs and recited poems. Mr. Johnston lit his pipe and . . ."

"What did you say?" Dad broke in.

I should have been warned by his tone and by the fact that he had interrupted me. But I rushed on, freely borrowing more details from the book.

"He tipped his chair back, put his feet on the desk, lit his pipe and. . ."

My father sat forward and slammed his hands down on the table.

"Lit his pipe!" he said, giving his chair a thrust backwards. "That school's a fire trap. I'm going to phone the chairman of the school board."

"No!" I shrieked. "No, don't!"

Dad paused and levelled a steely gaze at my flushed face. I could not meet his eyes.

"Well, did he smoke or didn't he? Which is it to be? I want the truth."

"She's lying," Hugh put in. "She always lies."

I turned on him, hoping he would divert Dad's attention.

"I do not lie," I cried. "I don't. You . . ."

"Jean, I am waiting for an answer to a question," Dad said as if Hugh had not spoken. "Did your teacher smoke a pipe or didn't he? Yes or no? It's as simple as that."

I knew it was not simple at all. If I said he did not smoke, the next question would be why had I lied. Yet if I stuck to my story, Dad would make that phone call and Mr. Johnston would be in trouble.

"He had a pipe," I faltered, doing my best to save both myself and my teacher, "but I don't think he lit it."

"But you are quite sure he had a pipe in his mouth?"

"I think he did. Somebody said..."

"Are you telling me now that you yourself never saw a pipe, that you are merely repeating what somebody said?"

The minute I nodded, my father shot another question at me. "Who said this?"

I shrank lower in my chair.

"Jean knows now that she was mistaken, don't you?" Mother intervened.

"Telling a lie about a man like Don Johnston is more serious than merely being mistaken," my father grumbled.

"Llew, I think you've made your point," she said, smiling a little. "Very effectively, too, I may say."

Dad stopped glaring at her and grinned.

"Thank you," he said, drawing his chair up to the table again. Ignoring me, he began to eat his meatloaf.

I did not tell him another lie for at least a week.

One day I had my first headache. As life at school went on being difficult, I had them more and more frequently. I also chewed my tongue. And my hair began to fall out. Soon I had a bald spot the size of a fifty-cent-piece on one side of my head. My parents made an appointment with a skin specialist in Toronto.

The morning we were to go, Mother wakened me before it was light outside. She turned on the lamp that hung over the head of my bed.

"Stay where you are," she said with a shiver. "The house is still too cold for you to get up quite yet. I've brought you an orange to eat in bed. When you finish, put on your dressing gown and come to the kitchen. It's warmer there. You can get dressed after breakfast."

She helped me sit up and handed me a plate. She had cut an orange into sections, each still with its skin on. You picked them up and ate the fruit off the peel. She called them boats. On the plate was a small fleet of them.

When she went away, I lined the bright little boats up, one behind the other, on the windowsill beside me. The world outside was dark, and the wood of the windowsill was a mahogany brown. The orange segments glowed against the sombre background. I loved the look of them. I could hardly bear to spoil it by eating one.

As I took the one farthest away and began to chew the pulp, I realized with a pang that in a week, even in a day, maybe, I would have forgotten how beautiful that line of glowing orange boats looked. I could not remember moments like this in the week that had just passed. Nobody but me had seen the fleet on my windowsill. In a few minutes I would have eaten them and only flattened bits of rind would be left.

It is part of my life, I thought, trying to work out what was bothering me, and I am forgetting it. This is something that is just mine. If I forget it, it will be as if it never happened.

I sat very still, no longer eating, struggling with a thought almost beyond my own understanding. Yet I did recognize, in that small space of time, that it was up to me to hold onto such memories.

I straightened my shoulders, stared at the brave little fleet and spoke aloud.

"I will remember, as long as I live, how these orange boats look right now," I vowed solemnly.

Feeling exalted, I began to eat. I did not make a vow to treasure up *all* such moments. I knew, even though I was only nine, that I could not manage that, however hard I tried. But I determined to do my best to remember more. I would hold onto special moments and ordinary, everyday ones, too.

The skin specialist said he thought my dermititis might be caused by stress. He gave Mother sticky ointment to use on my scalp, and he said my hair would grow again. It did.

His diagnosis was not what made that day important, though. And neither was my memory of the fleet of orange boats a particularly significant one. What mattered was that for the first time I saw my world and my life as something that belonged to me, and began to put small scraps of time away in a place where I could take them out and look at them whenever I needed to remember.

❧ 13 ❧

I looked up from my grade five reader and smiled. I liked Miss Marr a lot. And, even though we had only met an hour ago, I thought she liked me, too.

She was young and pretty and she had a gentle voice. But that was not all. Like Mr. Johnston, she had had polio. As I listened to her passing out books behind me, I could hear her limping, first a quick step, then a slow one. The sound made me feel a little less lonely. My teacher would understand how it felt to be the only cross-eyed girl in Victory School.

"This is your desk, Jean," she had said.

It sat, all by itself, right up against the front blackboard. I was supposed to be able to see better there. I had not yet managed to make anyone understand that if I wanted to read what was written on the board, I would have to stand up so that my face was only inches away from the writing. Then I would have to walk back and forth, following the words not only with my eyes but with my entire body. If the writing were up at the top of the board, I would have to stand on tiptoe or even climb on a chair to be able to decipher it. If it were near the bottom, I would have to crouch down.

I remembered Miss Bogart printing large, thick, yellow letters on a green chalkboard. That had been so different. These dusty grey boards looked almost the same colour as the thin, white scratches Miss Marr's chalk made. Her small, neat words were composed of letters that flowed into each other, too, which made reading them even harder.

I would not explain. How could I? She might make me climb and crouch to read the words.

I stood out far too much as it was. All the desks except mine were nailed to the floor in five straight rows. The seats flipped up when you slid out of them. They were attached to the desk behind. On top was a trough for your pencil and, in the right-hand corner, an inkwell which Miss Marr kept filled from a big ink bottle with a long spout. All the desk lids were a dark wine colour.

My desk was new and varnished a shiny golden brown. It had been provided for me because, in theory, it could be moved to wherever I could see best. It was, however, far too heavy and unwieldy for Miss Marr or me to shift. All that special desk did was single me out even more.

I turned sideways in my new desk so that I could watch Miss Marr and caught sight of Shirley Russell instead. If only she would notice me!

Shirley had about her the magic of a story. She and her brother Ian had come from England to stay with their aunt and uncle and be safe from the bombing. She had joined our class near the end of grade four. Shirley had a lovely voice, with an accent like the child movie actress Margaret O'Brien's. She also had golden ringlets, longer and fairer than Shirley Temple's. She was a War Guest. She was different, too, but everybody wanted to be her friend.

"Face front, Jean," Miss Marr said. "Here are your spelling words."

She had typed them for me on a big print typewriter. I bent over them, drawing each letter on the roof of my mouth with the tip of my tongue. I had discovered that this helped me to remember them. It also helped fill in time.

When the bell rang for recess, Miss Marr astonished me by saying to Shirley Russell, "This is Jean Little, Shirley. She can't see well. Would you be her friend and help her get into the right line when it's time to come back inside?"

Shirley smiled sweetly and nodded her golden head. I could not believe this was really happening. Shirley Russell was actually going to be my friend. At last I was going to have a girl to do things with, and not just any girl. The War Guest herself!

We marched down the stairs and went out into the girls' side of the playground. I turned to Shirley, my smile shy, my heart singing.

Shirley scowled. Just under her breath, so that nobody but me could hear, she snarled, "You keep away from me. Get lost!"

Then she turned and ran.

"Be my partner, Shirley, and I'll give you my Crackerjack prize," I heard one girl call out.

There was a hubbub of offered bribes and vows of eternal friendship. Nobody looked in my direction.

I stood where I was, stunned into immobility. I should have guessed, perhaps, that our teacher had asked the impossible of the English girl. She was popular at the moment, but if she had me trailing after her, her accent might suddenly cease to be interesting and just be weird. She was a foreigner, after all, and she knew it.

Before any of them had time to notice me watching them, I walked away to the far side of the playground. I leaned up against a tall tree and stared off into the distance, as though I had my mind on things other than silly grade five girls. To keep myself from crying, I began talking to the tree that was supporting me.

"Are you lonely, too, tree?" I murmured. "If you are, I'll come every day and talk to you. We could be friends."

As I drew a shaking breath, much like a sob, I heard a gentle rustle above my head. I glanced up. The leafy branches seemed to nod to me.

You can count on a tree, I told myself. A tree is better than a person.

But I knew it was not true.

Me, aged 10, with our dog Chummy
(Chummy didn't notice I was different.)

When we were supposed to line up to march in again, I heard Shirley's laugh and tagged on the end of the right line. I counted my steps on the way in. I'd find it tomorrow without any help from Shirley Russell.

Back at my desk, I heard Miss Marr ask two people to pass out pieces of paper. Staring down at the blank sheet, I hoped we were going to draw or write a composition.

"We're going to have a mental arithmetic test," Miss Marr said. "Write down the numbers 1 to 10 on your paper."

I bent my arm around my sheet, shielding it from prying eyes, even though the others were not close to me. I had a sinking feeling the test she was talking about would involve those horrible times tables everybody but me had mastered in grade three. I picked up the special fat pencil Miss Marr had given me and did as I had been told. As I waited for the first question, I clutched the pencil so tightly that my knuckles whitened.

"Question one," said Miss Marr. "8 × 3."

I began to add. Eight and eight were. . . sixteen? Or was it fourteen?

Three and three are six, I muttered inside my head, changing my method of attack. I turned down two fingers so that I would know when I reached eight.

"Question two," Miss Marr said. "6 × 4."

I gave up on question one and began to add fours. I had reached twelve and four are sixteen when she went on to question three.

When she reached question ten, I stared down at my paper in dismay. All that was written on it were the numbers 1 to 10 in a neat column. I had not managed to get even one answer.

"Since this is the first day, you can each mark your own paper," she said. "What is it, Ruth?"

"Can I sharpen my pencil?" Ruth Dayton's voice asked.

"Yes. But hurry up. You are keeping us all waiting."

As she passed behind me, Ruth glanced over my shoulder. I did not notice her small hiss of astonishment as she took in the fact that I had not answered a single question.

"The answer to question one is twenty-four," the teacher said as Ruth regained her seat.

I knew that behind my back, forty pencils were checking the answer. I had to do something to look busy. With painstaking neatness, I pencilled in 24 beside the number 1.

"If you have 24 beside the number 1," said my new teacher, "check it right."

I stared down at my page. There, right next to the 1 was written 24. Feeling a little like a sleepwalker, unable to stop herself, I put a check mark next to the answer my teacher had just dictated. After all, she had *not* said, "If you got the answer right . . . " She had said, "If you have the number 24 beside the number 1 . . ." And I did.

"The correct answer for Number 2 is also 24," she said then. I wrote that down.

"If you have the answer 24 beside the number 2, check it right."

We worked our way down the sheet. First she would tell us the answer. I would write it down. Then she would instruct us to "check it right," and I would put a neat check mark on the paper.

When the others had finished marking their answers right or wrong, Miss Marr said, "Raise your hand if you have ten answers checked right."

I looked at my arithmetic paper. There they were, all ten answers checked right. I raised my hand. As I did so, I expected something dramatic to happen, a thunderbolt to strike me dead or a huge voice to roar, *"Jean Little, what have you done?"* Nothing of the kind disturbed Miss Marr's classroom. The teacher looked around at the eight or nine raised hands.

"Good for you," she said.

I snatched my hand down and stared hard at a broken piece of chalk lying in the chalk trough. I did not check to see whether anybody admitted to having none checked right. I was sure I was the only one who would have missed them all.

As she began a geography lesson, I felt relief wash over me. Mental arithmetic was at an end, for that day, at least. Perhaps everything was going to be all right.

My happiness lasted until noon.

Ruth and Stella came marching up to my desk while I was putting away my books. They stared at me with contempt.

"I saw you," Ruth said.

"What a cheat!" Stella put in. Her eyes were gleaming.

"Saw me what?" I said feebly. "I don't know what you're talking about. I didn't cheat."

"You might as well save your breath," Stella sneered. Ruth *saw* you and so did I. You copied down the answers after she said them out loud."

"Are you going to tell on me?" I heard, and despised, the bleat of panic in my voice. They had me at their mercy and we all knew it.

"Do you think we would tattle?" Stella said, as though such a thing had never been known to happen. "We won't tell."

I cheered up too soon. She had not finished.

"But if you don't tell her yourself what a cheater you are, nobody in this class will ever speak to you again. We don't intend to be friends with a cheater."

I had no choice. I longed for friends. In spite of Shirley's snub, I still hoped that someday it might happen. I couldn't risk turning the entire class against me.

Miss Marr was at her desk. I walked up to stand beside it, moving slowly, trying hard to think of a way to confess that would satisfy my class and not make Miss Marr hate me.

Ruth and Stella lurked near enough to hear what I said. I stood by my teacher's elbow until she looked up. Then I took a deep breath and began. I stammered and stuttered, but at last she took in what I was mumbling. She told me to sit down. Then she waved Stella and Ruth away.

"You two are supposed to be on your way home," she said, her voice a little sharp. "Run along."

They went as slowly as they dared, but until they were well out of earshot, Miss Marr ignored me. She sharpened a pencil, then two. Finally she turned and looked at me.

"I saw what you did, Jean," she said.

I gasped. Had she watched me cheat and said nothing? I could not believe it.

She sat down near me and went on quietly.

"I don't think you meant to cheat, did you? It just happened . . . when you could not get the answers fast enough to keep up. Wasn't that the way it was?"

"Yes. That's just what happened," I told her, staring at the floor and trying not to cry. "I'm no good at my times tables . . ."

"You won't ever do it again, will you?"

I shook my head violently.

"Never ever!"

"Then we'll just forget it this time," she told me. "And you'd better get busy learning your tables."

"I will," I promised. "Oh, I will."

I positively ran from the room. But when I got outside, I found Ruth and Stella and four or five others waiting.

"What did she say?" they demanded.

I opened my mouth to tell them how nice Miss Marr had been. Then I stopped to think. The minute the other kids found out that I had not got the strap or been sent to the principal, they would all decide she was a "soft" teacher, easy to put one over on.

"I won't tell you," I said as bravely as I could, "but she was mad!"

Ruth seemed impressed. Stella gave me a scornful glance. But as she reached out to grab my hand and turn it palm up to see if it had strap marks on it, Jamie came around the corner of the school. He glanced in our direction, was about to go on, and then turned back.

"What's going on?" he demanded.

"He's my brother," I told them, feeling as though Robin Hood himself had come to my rescue.

The girls backed away.

"We're not hurting her," Ruth declared, but she was moving off step by step.

The rest melted away without a word. Jamie gave

me an annoyed, big-brotherly look.

"You'd better hurry up or you'll be late for dinner," he said. "You can't walk with me."

I smiled. "I know," I told him humbly.

I knew better than to expect an eighth grade boy to walk with a mere fifth grade girl. Yet just knowing he was in the world, I felt protected all the way home.

⚘ 14 ⚘

I was eating my porridge when Hugh, hurrying too fast, fell down the back stairs. Before Mother could get up, he limped in, sniffling slightly, and displayed a bumped elbow for her inspection. Mother examined it gravely.

"A slight haematoma," she said in a serious voice. "And an abrasion almost invisible to the naked eye. You'll live."

Hugh, who always recovered with the speed of light and who won Mother's admiration with his bravery, chuckled at the impressive words.

"What does that mean?" he asked.

"A little bruise and a scrape I can hardly see."

I glowered at my oatmeal. Why did she have to smile at him like that? He was not so special. I searched my mind for something terrible he had done that I could tell her about.

"Jean, hurry up or you'll be late," Grandma said.

I did not want to go to school. We were going to have another mental arithmetic test, and I still did not know my times tables. If only I could fall down and break my leg . . .

Four-year-old Pat grinned at me.

"Huwwy up, Jean," she parroted. "You'll be late."

I wanted to slap the wide smile off her silly little face. Instead I scooped up a few drops of milk on the tip of my spoon and let fly. The tiny bit of milk splashed her on the nose. I laughed. Before anyone could stop her, Pat grabbed up her mug filled to the brim with milk and sent its entire contents sloshing over me, soaking me to the skin.

The next thing I knew, I was back upstairs changing out of my wet serge dress, cotton petticoat, long brown stockings and underwear into clean dry clothes. Not only was this going to make me really late, but Mother handed me the knitted suit Aunt Gretta had made for my tenth birthday. The ribbed blue skirt was sewn onto a sleeveless cotton vest. Over it went a horizontally striped blue and pink sweater with short sleeves. Nobody else in Miss Marr's class had a homemade knitted suit anything like it.

"I can't wear it," I said in anguished tones.

"It's lovely," my mother said calmly. "Gretta worked hard to make it for you. Don't be ridiculous. Of course you will wear it."

In ten minutes I was gobbling toast and honey, gulping down milk and hating my cheerful little sister who was the cause of all the trouble and who got to stay home and be spoiled by everybody.

When I reached the street, it was ominously quiet. I really was going to be late, and it was all Pat's fault. I ran the first three blocks, but slowed down when I got a stitch in my side. There was still not a single child in sight.

As I passed St. John's School, I could hear the grade four class singing "God Save the King." I sent the small building a look of longing. Mr. Johnston had not had these horrid mental arithmetic tests.

Then I stood stock still. When I got to school, Miss Marr would tell me to put my name on the board to stay after four. I didn't mind staying late — lots of the others got detentions — I wasn't sure what to write, though I had a strong suspicion that you did not write out your whole name. Did you just write your initials? Or one initial and your surname? Or your first name and your last initial?

I had to get it right. The others still called me names when no teacher was near enough to hear. The only game I had ever been invited to play was Crack the Whip, and they always made me go on the end. Then, when the big girl at the front swung everybody around in a long *Crack!*, I ended up flying through the air and landing with a jarring crash on my hands and knees. As I picked myself up, I'd try to look as though I thought crash-landings were fun. Nobody was fooled.

If I wrote my name up there differently than the others did, they would have a new thing to tease me about. I could hear the jeering voices already.

"You're not just cross-eyed, you're so *dumb* you don't even know how to write your name on the board!"

I stood there, thinking hard. How could I save myself? Once in awhile, when a child brought a note from home, he got out of putting his name on the board. Well, my mother would not write me a note.

Perhaps, if your parents were not at home, and some emergency cropped up and you had to deal with it, Miss Marr just might let you sit down without asking for a note. It would have to be a desperate emergency . . .

I began to walk again, taking my time. I had to invent the most convincing lie of my life. Bit by bit, I worked it out. As I imagined how it must have happened, it grew so real that I began to believe it myself. I had every detail ready as I turned the last corner. Then I began to run.

I knew it was essential that I be out of breath when I arrived.

I dashed up the stairs, puffing hard. I opened the door, said a private prayer for help, and entered the grade five classroom. Miss Marr was at her desk. Out of the corner of my eye, I could see monitors collecting the test papers. So far so good.

"Jean," said my teacher, "you're late."

"Yes," I panted, facing her and opening my eyes wide so that I would look innocent and pitiful. "I know. I couldn't help it."

"Why are you late?" she asked.

I took a deep breath.

"Well, I was all ready in plenty of time. But just as I was going out the door, the telephone rang. I knew I should not go back to answer it, but you know my mother and father are both doctors and I was afraid it might be an emergency."

Miss Marr opened her mouth to ask a question, but I rushed on, not giving her time to get a word in edgewise.

"The trouble was, you see, that nobody was home but me. So I took the receiver off the hook and I said, 'Dr. Littles' residence.' "

Everybody was listening now, even the boys who never paid attention. I kept going.

"MY DAUGHTER IS DYING! MY DAUGHTER IS DYING!"

I saw my teacher jump as I shrieked the words at the top of my lungs. Her eyes were wide with shock. The class gasped. I did not stop for effect. I could not give the teacher time to interrupt.

"It was a man's voice. He sounded frantic with

worry. 'I'm sorry,' I told him, 'my parents are out. If you call back, they should be home in one hour.' 'No! Please, don't hang up,' he begged. 'You must come and save her life. If I wait for your parents, she will surely die.' 'Well, I guess if she is dying, I'd better come. Where do you live?' I asked him. '111 King Street,' he told me.''

Miss Marr did not even try to ask a question as I paused to catch my breath. The entire class was sitting spellbound. The silence was absolute. Not a desk seat squeaked. Not a giggle broke the hush.

"I hurried in and got the right medicine from the office and then I ran out the door. I didn't go the long way around by the Norwich Street bridge. I was afraid it would take too long. I went down London Road and across some stepping stones down there. When I got to King Street, there was the house. It was a log cabin with wind whistling through the cracks. And as I came up to it, I saw the door was standing open and there were a bunch of people in the doorway and they were all crying. 'What's wrong?' I asked them. 'You are too late,' they sobbed. 'She's dead already.' ''

This time, as I snatched a breath, Miss Marr choked back a small sound. She made no attempt to stem the flood of my story. I pressed on.

" 'Oh, I am so sorry,' I told them. 'Take me to see her.' So they took me into the cabin and there lay the girl on a trundle bed. Her face was blue and her eyes had rolled up till you could just see white and her teeth were clenched. And her fingers and toes all curled over backwards.''

I watched Miss Marr carefully at this point, because I was not absolutely sure what a dead person looked like. The last bit worried me especially. I had heard someone say that when people died, they turned their toes up. That could only mean that their toes curled over backwards, but I was not sure about the fingers.

Miss Marr's face quivered a little and her mouth twitched, but she did not speak. I hurried, eager to finish. It would be a relief to sit down. Even so, in spite of myself, I kept putting in extra bits as they occurred to me.

" 'She's not quite dead,' I cried. 'She's just on the point of death. I think I can save her.' I hit her chin and her mouth opened. I poured in the medicine. She fluttered her lashes and turned a normal colour and said weakly, 'Where am I?' I turned and hurried toward the door. But before I could escape, all the weeping people went down on their knees and grabbed hold of my skirt and they said, 'You saved her life! We want to give you a reward. Gold, silver, a bag of emeralds, a horse that will come when you whistle . . . tell us the one thing you want more than anything else in the world and you can have it.' "

I paused for effect this time. I knew no one would break the hush. I wanted my teacher to take in the next bit.

" 'The one thing I want more than anything else in the world,' I told them, 'is to be on time for school.' So they let me go and I ran down the hill and across the stepping stones. When I got to the third last stone, though, I slipped and fell in the river and cut my knee. I had to get to shore, go home and bandage my knee and put on dry clothes. Then I hurried here as fast as I could. And that is why I am late."

There was a stunned silence in the classroom. Miss Marr and I stared at each other for a long, long minute. I waited for her to tell me to write my name on the board. Instead she pointed her finger at my desk. Speaking extremely slowly and wearily, she said, "Take . . . your . . . seat. Just . . . take . . . your . . . seat."

I tried to keep a solemn expression on my face. But it was hard not to grin. I sat down and did not turn my head as a buzz of whispers broke out behind me. I had missed the mental arithmetic test. I had not had to write my name on the board. And I had kept every single person transfixed with my exciting story.

At least three blissful minutes went by before I realized I had no cut on my knee and no bandage, either. Not only that, but I could not remember whether I had told her which knee I was supposed to have cut.

She had believed me. I was sure of that. Yet any second she was going to discover that I had told her a stupendous lie.

I hooked one knee over the other and clasped my hands around the knee on top. I spent the entire morning that way. When I was required to write, I used only one hand. Miss Marr did not ask me a direct question. When recess time came and she said, "Class, stand," I stayed where I was.

"Jean, aren't you going out for recess?" she asked when the others had marched out and there I still sat.

"Oh, Miss Marr," I said in my smallest, most pathetic voice, "I am so tired from saving that girl's life that I have to stay in and have a rest."

Still clutching my knee with both hands, I laid my head down on my desk and shut my eyes.

She did not say a word.

At noon, when she had her back turned, I ran out of the classroom, dashed home, sneaked bandaids from my parents' office and plastered them over both knees, to be on the safe side. When I returned to school, Miss Marr smiled and did not ask why both my knees were bandaged.

I sat through the afternoon thinking over what had happened. Did she really guess? The other kids did not seem to have figured out that I had lied. One girl had even smiled at me, as though she might be my friend. Nobody in my class had called me cross-eyed. A boy in grade seven had, though. If only I could shut him up the way I had hushed everybody that morning.

Then I remembered Hugh's knee. That night I asked Mother, "What are the long words for what's wrong with my eyes?"

I was standing beside her chair. She looked up at me.

"Why?" she asked.

"I want to know, that's all. They call me cross-eyed. I want to know the long words, the ones doctors use."

She rhymed off a whole list.

"Say it again. Slowly."

"Strabismus, nystagmus, corneal opacities and eccentric pupils."

I practised.

The next day I was late coming out of school. The same grade-seven boy was waiting for me. He had his first snowball ready.

"Cross-eyed, cross-eyed," he chanted and waited for me to start running so that he could chase me, pelting me with hard-packed snowballs.

I turned on him instead.

"I am not cross-eyed," I said in a strong, clear

voice. "I have corneal opacities and eccentric pupils."

I glared at him as I spoke, and my eyes were as crossed as ever. But he was so surprised that he stood there, his mouth gaping open like a fish's.

Then I turned my back and walked away. Perhaps his aim was off because he was so used to firing his missiles at a running target. But the first snowball flew past me harmlessly. The second exploded with a smack against a nearby tree.

I kept walking, chin in the air.

In the last two days, I had learned a lot about the power of words. Snowballs would hit me again and I would run away and cry. I would be late and, eventually, I would even have to write my name on the board.

But I had found out what mere words could do. I would not forget.

❧ 15 ❧

"Holy, holy, holy," we sang. "Lord God Almighty . . ."

Mother's hand touched my arm, and I stopped swaying to the music. I pulled away with an impatient hunch of my shoulders. I felt peaceful as I swayed, until that hand stopped me and broke into the dreamy lullabye motion. I did not know I was doing it usually, but I hated being stopped.

I could not hang onto my irritation, though, not today. It was spring. Sunlight spilled through the stained-glass windows, splashing the people in the gallery with rainbow colours. And when our singing stopped, I could hear distant birds singing on.

I was also proud as a peacock in my new clothes. Mother had been given some white Chinese silk, and she had had a seamstress make a long-sleeved blouse for me. With it I wore a black velvet skirt with straps over my shoulders and a short black velvet jacket. I also had on a new hat with ribbons that hung down my back, long white stockings and shiny black strap shoes. The blouse felt cool and soft against my arms, and I stroked the velvet with an appreciative fingertip. I felt elegant.

If only I didn't have to sit still and be good, this day would be perfect.

Then I remembered that Dad had joined the Navy and gone to war. I should be worrying about him. I ought to be sad. The War did not seem real to me, though. When we went to the movies on Saturday afternoons, we always saw a newsreel. I had even seen Hitler himself, small and yelling and waving his arms, and watched people giving the *Heil Hitler* salute and cheering. I had cried over the movie *Journey for Margaret*, all about this poor little girl whose family had been killed by bombs. We gave half our allowance to help buy War Savings Stamps, and we collected old tin cans and glass bottles and the silk from milkweed pods to help win The War.

So The War was all around me. But until Dad got into the Navy and went away, it made me excited more than sad.

Mother did not think it was exciting, though. I knew that. She did not get all upset the way some of the other mothers did. She scolded us if she heard us saying Germans were bad. When ladies came to tea and sounded sorry for Mother, she said Dad was only working on a naval base in Halifax.

I allowed myself to enjoy the lovely spring day again. In our family we stayed calm. We did not fuss. Not as long as Dad was still safe in Canada, anyway.

It was then that I heard Grandma gasp.

I turned to stare at her, even though we were supposed to be praying. She looked agitated.

"Amen," said the minister.

At once, Grandma leaned over Jamie and whispered something into Mother's ear. Mother's lips twitched.

"It's all right," I heard her murmur back. "We've only been gone ten minutes."

Then she leaned across Hugh and whispered to me, "Jean, slip out quietly down the side aisle and go home and turn the heat off under the rice. Grandma left it on and it mustn't boil dry."

I could not believe it.

"Scoot," she urged, and as I started to get up, she added with a grin of understanding, "You needn't come back. We'll be home when church is over."

I stepped out the front door of Chalmers Church into a glorious, sunny April morning. As I stood there breathing in the intoxicating scent of fresh damp earth and beginning to taste the sweetness of unexpected freedom, I heard them start on the second hymn.

> For the beauty of the earth,
> For the beauty of the skies . . .

I hummed the tune softly as I walked very quietly the length of the first block. Then, as I passed Knox Church, I pulled off my hat and, swinging it by its elastic, started to skip. Everybody in the world was in church, and I was free. The thought of all those people sitting still while I skipped along filled me with added rapture.

As I sped past St. Andrew's church, I realized that part of the magic of the morning lay in the fact that nobody in the whole world knew exactly where I was or what I was doing. Mother could guess, but what if I turned the corner and went home by a different way? She would never know. I was in complete control.

Then I remembered the pot beginning to boil dry. I hurried.

As I ran the last half block, I glanced at the First Baptist church directly across the street from our house. As if on signal the people inside started to sing. They were so close to me and yet I did not know any of them. This thought made me uneasy. Until this moment I had been sure that I, myself, was the one person that God looked after with extra special care. Could it be that those Baptists meant as much to God as I and the other members of my family?

Turning in at our walk, I forgot them and went into the house. It sounded too quiet and empty. I hurried down the hall to the kitchen, making as much noise as possible. I switched off the burner.

Then I dashed up to my room, stretched out on my bed without giving a thought to my lovely new clothes, and went on reading *Jane of Lantern Hill*. I had had to leave it when it was time to go to church. I had been upset because I was about to begin the last chapter and I wanted to know how it would all turn out. I had thought I would not be able to finish till after dinner. Now I had this gift of time.

I finished it just as the rest of the family came trooping in. Grandma kissed me for being so good and going home to fix things. Hugh and Jamie gave me glances of pure envy.

That afternoon I almost wished that I had not finished my book. Now I wanted a new story to read. I thought over the books we owned. We had lots of them, more than any other children I knew. But I wanted something new and different, something as good as *Lassie Come Home*.

I wandered through the house, unable to settle. When I came into my own room, I saw the new school supplies Mother had got for me. I sat down at my table and handled them lovingly. Three new Eberhard 2B pencils, a fat pink eraser and an orange scribbler with black writing on the front. I had sharpened the pencils already. I opened the notebook to its first, inviting blank page.

Idly, not really planning what I was about to do, I

picked up one of my new pencils and began to write.

There was once a boy who lived in a shack on the top of a high mountain. He lived there with his mother and his brave and beautiful collie dog named Lad. One day, the boy found his mother lying on the floor unconscious. "Mother, speak to me!" cried the boy. But the mother just lay still with her eyes closed. Her face was deathly pale. "Lad," said the boy to the brave dog at his side, "we will have to go for the doctor."

My pencil flew across page after page. Lad and his master went through a raging blizzard, across a burning desert, past a fierce grizzly bear, across a raging waterfall. I stopped at that word and remembered that the blizzard had also been raging. I crossed out the second "raging" and put "foaming" instead. I did not know that, in that instant, I had started to turn into a writer.

"Jean, we're going for a walk," Mother called from the foot of the back stairs.

"I'm busy. Do I have to come?" I called back.

"What are you busy at?" she asked.

I did not want to explain. The boy was staggering into the village, searching everywhere for the doctor.

"It's private," I said. "But it's important. A kind of secret."

"All right," she said. "We won't be gone long. Grandma's having a rest. Try not to disturb her."

I wrote on, praying that Grandma would not wake up and disturb *me*. When Mother was not around to protect us, Grandma liked to keep us busy. "The devil finds work for idle hands," was how she put it.

I had a feeling that, in Grandma's opinion, writing a story might well be the devil's work. Especially if you did it for pleasure, on Sunday.

The boy finally found the doctor in a tavern. The doctor did not want to come at first because night was falling.

"Lad and I will guide you," said the boy.

As the three of them struggled back over the perilous route the boy and dog had taken earlier, the ground shook beneath their feet.

I had remembered the earthquakes in Taiwan. I might as well put one in.

As soon as my family returned, Pat came running to see what I was doing. She loved secrets. I pushed her out the door, even though the room was hers as much as mine.

"I'm busy," I snarled. Seeing her face pucker up and her mouth start to open in a wail, I changed my tone. Wheedling sometimes worked, especially if it were accompanied by a bribe.

"Don't cry or tell," I said hastily, "and as soon as I'm done, I'll show you. I'm writing a story."

Her eyes grew bright. She loved stories. She knew I could read them aloud or tell them because I did both all the time. But she had not realized before that I could also write them. She backed up and allowed me to shut the door.

I listened. Was she going to run and tell? There was a small thud outside. My sister had sat herself down, her back against the bedroom door, to wait.

I wrote on. My hand ached. The printing on the page grew sloppier by the minute.

But I wouldn't have stopped of my own free will for anything. Even gold, silver, a bag of emeralds or a horse that would come when you whistled.

> The mother blinked her eyes. "Where am I?"
> she asked. The boy slumped to the floor, spent
> and exhausted. The dog sat by his master's limp
> body, guarding him. "If it weren't for this brave
> boy and his noble dog," the doctor said to the
> mother, "you would now be dead."

"And so," I wrote, *"they all lived happily ever after."*
I had to end it abruptly that way because I had
filled the entire scribbler with my story and I, like my
unconscious hero, was "spent and exhausted."

Leaning back in my chair, I flipped through the
pages. There was the part about the bears. And there
was the earthquake.

I had written a book!

It wasn't a real book. Real books had chapters and
more people. *Jane of Lantern Hill* was a real book. But
writing this story had been as exciting for me as
reading.

And someday I would write a real one. When I
could type as fast as Miss Marr, maybe. Real writers
typed.

"Is the story done yet?" asked a small, hopeful
voice from the other side of the door.

I jumped up, weariness forgotten. She wanted to
hear my story. Everybody would want to hear it.
Hugh would like the dog. They would *all* like the dog.

"It is finished," I cried joyfully, pulling the door
open so quickly that she toppled into the room.
"Come on. I want to read it out loud to Mum and Dad,
too."

"Daddy's gone away to the Navy," Pat said.

For me, that was the moment when the war really began.

Me, age 12, on a family holiday *(Mother took pictures to send to Dad, who was in the Navy.)*

☙ 16 ☙

In the fall I went into Miss Ibbotson's class. We had to learn about decimals and percents. I disliked grade six till the day Miss Ibbotson started us writing journals.

When she passed out the notebooks, they did not look special. They had blue paper covers and lined pages with a thin red margin. I could not see those faint lines when I was writing.

"For the last half hour, every day this month," Miss Ibbotson told us, "you will keep a diary. You will write in them what happened in your life that day and how you felt."

She talked on for a few minutes, but I was not listening. I could hardly wait to begin.

That first afternoon, I did write down what had actually happened in my life that day. I may even have stuck to the truth till page three or four. But long before the first week was up, I had begun fancying things up a little.

My real life was simply too dull to be worth recording.

I began stealing ideas from a book we had at home called *Boyhood Stories of Famous Men*. In the book one boy saved the day by carving a lion out of butter to be used as a decoration for the King's table. Another made his own paints by crushing berries and boiling roots, and little Wolfgang Mozart and his big sister went to perform on the harpsichord before the child Marie Antoinette. The book went on to explain how each boy later became famous.

I liked the story about the young Mozart best. What drew me to it was his older sister. She was shown in the illustration, standing behind Wolfgang and the pretty little princess. I knew exactly how she must be feeling. She, too, was a gifted musician, but her little brother was the hero of the story. It never said what happened to her.

In my journal, I had myself carving wonderful animals, playing the piano brilliantly before I was five and making my own paints.

One day's entry read like this:

> Last night, a famous artist came to have supper at our house. Mother took him down to the cellar. The great painter stopped dead in his tracks and pointed to our cellar walls.
>
> "Madam," he cried, "whoever painted these magnificent murals on your walls?"
>
> Mother stared at the wondrous paintings.
>
> "I have no idea," she said in a bewildered voice. She turned to her children.
>
> "Children," she said, "have you any idea who painted these magnificent murals?"
>
> The other children shook their heads.
>
> "As a matter of fact," I said, "I painted them."
>
> "But you had no paints!" Mother cried.
>
> "I know," I said modestly, "but I so longed to paint that I boiled roots and squeezed berries and made my own paints."
>
> The great artist patted my head.
>
> "Madam," he said, with tears in his eyes, "someday this little girl of yours will be world famous as an artist."

Each afternoon when the bell rang and Miss Ibbotson told us to put the books away, I emerged from my fantasy life reluctantly. All day I looked forward to three-fifteen.

Then one afternoon, instead of telling us to put our books away, Miss Ibbotson told us to hand them in.

I was horrified. It had never crossed my mind that Miss Ibbotson planned to read our journals. I thought diaries were private.

The teacher was going to read all those stories. What if she called my mother and asked her for the name of the famous artist?

For days after, whenever the phone rang, I braced myself. But Miss Ibbotson did not call.

Then she gave our diaries back. Before she let us have them, she stood and glared at us.

"I have never, in my whole life, read such rubbish," she growled. Then, in a high-pitched, mimicking voice, she pretended to read from one.

"Today is Monday. I got up at seven-thirty. I got dressed. I had breakfast. I went to school. We had arithmetic. We had spelling. We had recess . . ."

She pretended to turn a page. She squeaked on.

"Today is Tuesday. I got up at seven-thirty. I got dressed. I had breakfast. I went to school. We had arithmetic. We had spelling . . ."

We sat and stared at her. Wasn't that what she had wanted? She had told us to tell about our lives, hadn't she? Well, what she had just read out *was* how our lives went.

"I have never been more bored," declared our teacher. Then she looked at me. I shrank down in my seat.

"The only diary that I enjoyed reading was Jean Little's," Miss Ibbotson said slowly and distinctly. "Hers was at least entertaining. I shall never assign journal writing to a class again. Sylvia, pass out the books."

I sat there dazed. She had liked it. Not only that, she had liked it best. Yet mine had been a bunch of lies almost from start to finish.

As my journal smacked down on the lid of my desk and I caught the baleful look on Sylvia's face, I knew the teacher had not helped me in my search for friends. But I didn't care. I wanted to hug my blue book. I had entertained Miss Ibbotson. That was far more important than being good at decimals and percents.

Real writers kept diaries. I would become a writer.

As I walked home, I thought about books I might write. Perhaps I should write one called "Girlhood Stories of Famous Women." No. I wanted instead to tell about the big sisters who stood at the back of the picture and had to put up with famous little brothers. I knew how they felt.

In December, Dad came home on leave. At first we hung around him, all clamouring for attention.

Hugh got it when he said, "We got up one morning and there was a snowman in the yard. Guess who made it?"

"You?" Dad said, sitting down to listen.

"No," I interrupted, wanting to tell it properly.

"Let Hugh finish," my father said, reaching out to pull me onto the arm of his chair but still watching Hugh.

"Mother made it!" Hugh said excitedly.

Dad looked confused. Mother laughed. She sounded a bit flustered.

"I came home from the hospital at three in the morning," she explained, straightening a pile of magazines. "I wasn't a bit sleepy. And there was all this fresh snow and a full moon. . ."

I could not keep quiet another second.

"We went to bed," I burst out, "and there wasn't a snowman. And when we came down in the morning. . ."

"There *was* a snowman!" Hugh yelled.

"Have mercy on our eardrums," my mother said. I saw her glance at Dad. "I did wonder if any of our neighbours were looking out their windows," she added.

My father began to laugh. We were all pleased. But I knew I could have told it far better if they had let me.

A couple of days later, I came into the living room late in the afternoon and found my father sitting all by himself. He was reading the paper. I seldom had one of my parents to myself, because there were so many people in our house.

But now here he was.

"Dad, would you like me to sing for you?" I asked.

"Not just now, Jean," he said, without even looking up from the paper.

"Would you like me to dance for you?" I inquired. I did not know any dances, but I had just read *Ballet Shoes* and I thought I could improvise the way Posy Fossil did.

"No," he mumbled and continued reading.

I stared at the back of his paper. Eatons wanted you to do your Christmas shopping there.

Perhaps I should try poetry. I knew he liked poems. He had given me books of poetry for Christmas and my birthday. I liked poems, too. And I knew several by heart. But I did not feel hopeful as I asked if he wanted to hear me recite one.

"Uh-uh," he grunted and turned to the next section.

I wandered disconsolately up to the room I shared with Pat. She was out with Mother, so I had it to myself. I went to the window and stood looking out at the sunset. It was a vivid one that lifted my drooping spirits with its glorious banners of orange and yellow, its streak of purple.

If they put it in a book, I thought, it would sound unreal.

Then, turning away from the window, I saw blank paper and a pencil lying on the table I used as a desk.

I could write about it myself, I thought, sitting down and picking up the pencil. There were only three sheets of paper. Whatever I wrote must not be too long.

A poem, I thought. I could maybe write a poem.

The first line was easy.

"Orange flags are flying," I wrote. Then the next line wrote itself, and the next and the next.

Orange flags are flying,
No overhanging grey
Dims the rosy sunset
At the close of day.

I stared down at the page in incredulous delight. I could do it. I was a poet. It wasn't hard. And it satisfied something in me, something that would not have felt the same if I had written, "The clouds at sunset look like orange flags. There is no grey cloud to dim their brightness."

I went on eagerly, excited by what I was creating.

Royal purple nestles
'Round the golden clouds.

I paused to find a rhyme for "clouds." I could not think of a single one. Louds. Souds. They weren't even words. If I'd written "cloud," there were lots. Plowed. Loud. Bowed.

I could change it to "cloud."

Royal purple nestles
'Round the golden cloud.
And the windblown poplars
Before their Maker bowed.

There was something wrong with it. Part of it sounded as though it was happening now and part of it as though it happened yesterday. Never mind. I liked those poplars. I knew poplar trees by their shape. They were the only trees I could recognize that way. They lifted up their branches instead of bowing them, really, but never mind that, either.

O'er the snowy landscape,
Christmas bells ring out,
While, in nearby doorways,
Happy children shout.

I could hardly wait to show it to somebody. I had written three verses. But it did not sound finished. I had to put an end on it.

I chewed my pencil and stared into space. Then I had it.

> Many busy people
> Their tiresome work take leave
> To hurry home and welcome
> This year's Christmas Eve.

I read it over. I'd have to fix it. But first I wanted Dad to see it. Holding it up so that I could read it over while I walked along, I started to go back to where my father was sitting.

No. It looked too messy. He didn't like messy things. Besides, my poem deserved better than that.

I sat down again, took a fresh sheet of paper and copied it out. I changed "nestle" to "nestled" so the whole verse was in the past. I changed "nearby" to "neighbouring." It sounded fancier. I made "over-hanging" into "o'erhanging." That was poetic. I smiled at "'Round." There were lots of words like those in the poems we read at school.

Then I took the poem down to the living room. Dad was still reading the paper. I drew a deep breath.

"Dad," I announced, my voice shaking, "I've written a poem."

My father dropped the newspaper. His head jerked up. The sheets of newspaper floated to the floor all askew. He paid absolutely no attention to them.

"A poem!" he exclaimed. "Let me see it."

He looked as excited as I felt. He thought writing a poem was important. Wonderful, even. Shyly, I placed the sheet of paper in his hand.

Slowly, carefully, respectfully, he read to himself

each word I had written. Then, just as slowly, carefully and respectfully, he read it out loud.

I basked in his pride in me, but I heard, too, that it was not quite right.

"I have to fix it a bit," I said.

"Well, of course you do," he said, not giving it back yet. "This is what poets call a first draft. Good poets work over their poems for days sometimes, till each word is perfect. This first line, for instance. It sounds like a 12th of July parade."

What on earth was he talking about? He smiled at my baffled expression.

"That's the day the Orangemen parade," he said. "I'm sorry. I didn't really mean it. But why not say, 'Orange clouds were drifting.' Then the tenses would agree."

He explained to me what I had already noticed. Then he took out his pen and crossed out my first line, writing his above it.

I wanted to hit him. He was crazy. I had seen flags flying, banners, streamers. Not orange clouds.

He had gone on to the next verse. All through my poem, he crossed out things and wrote in extra or different words. Sometimes I could not help but see that he was right. Yet he should not have changed my poem. It wasn't his; it was mine.

Then, as I reached out to snatch it back, he reached out, too, and pulled me onto his lap. I snuggled close. He rubbed his bristly cheek up and down against my smooth one.

"My Blithe Spirit is a poet," he said. "How wonderful! I would have liked to be a poet, Jeanie. I became a doctor instead, but I'm so proud of you. I'll love having a poet for my daughter."

I didn't mind any longer, his changing my words. He was pleased with me. My heart sang.

Besides, I could change it all back later.

🏒 17 🏒

The summer I was eleven, Mother sent me to camp.

"It's only for two weeks," she said. "You'll have a good time, you'll see."

I felt the way I had long ago in Hong Kong, when she had made me go back and play out the game of Drop the Handkerchief. I did not want to go to camp. The other campers wouldn't like me. I would be miserably homesick. If Mother really loved me, she would understand this and let me stay home.

But deep down, I knew that she did understand. That was why she was sending me. It was time I made friends with children who were not characters in books. She hoped camp would help.

Skipper was my counsellor. She took me to my cabin. There were several girls already there. They lounged on their bunks and stared at me without saying a word.

"I'll leave you to make friends with each other," said Skipper casually, leaving me to the mercy of my cabin mates.

I hesitated in the doorway, uncertain what to do next. Nobody spoke till Skipper was out of earshot.

Then, out of the shadows, one of the girls on a top bunk drawled, "Have you had the Curse?"

Had I had what? She could not really have asked me if I had been cursed. I blinked nervously and said, "What?"

"She hasn't," another voice said, sounding extremely grown-up and bored. "You can tell. She doesn't even know what we're talking about."

"You have to sleep over there then," said the first voice. "This side of the cabin is reserved for girls who have had the Curse."

I picked up my suitcase and lugged it to an empty bottom bunk. If she had asked me if I had started to menstruate, I would have known the answer. Mother had explained the whole process. She had never thought to tell me the slang words for it.

As I made my bunk with the sheets I had brought, I felt utterly forlorn. And I had to stay here for fourteen nights and fourteen days. In spite of all I could do to keep them back, two tears began sliding down my cheeks.

"She's crying!" one of my cabin mates told the others.

"Oh, my God, she must be homesick," said the bored voice wearily. She sounded disgusted.

I made no friends at camp. I was left behind when they went cabin visiting after Lights Out. I might have betrayed them by tripping over things. Secretly I was relieved not to be included. I hated disobeying rules. I wanted to be good.

By now I was more or less accepted at school. I still yearned for a close friend, but I no longer expected to find one. When I was not reading my way through the white card books at the library, I played with Pat.

One October evening, Mother said, "There's a C.G.I.T. meeting at the church tonight. You're old enough to join now. I think you should go."

I would not look at her.

"I don't want to."

"You'll have a good time. You'll make friends."

"They won't like me. Anyway, I don't want friends."

Mother did not argue. She did not have to. We both knew that just the night before, I had been weeping because of my friendless state.

"You will have friends someday. Wait and see," was the best comfort Mother had had to offer. She said so again.

"I don't want friends someday. I want them *now*!" I wailed. "Why did God make me cross-eyed? It's not fair."

Mother sighed. We had been over this so often.

"Jeanie, God didn't make you cross-eyed," she told me for the hundredth time. "I must have had an infection early in my pregnancy which damaged your eyes while they were being formed. But God didn't make it happen. What kind of a God would deliberately do that to an unborn child?"

"Well, then, why doesn't He fix it? If my eyes were normal, I'd have lots of friends."

"Because He doesn't interfere with the laws of nature, I suppose," my mother said slowly. "As for your eyes keeping you from having friends, it won't always be that way. You may find one tonight at the C.G.I.T. meeting."

"I won't go," I said. "You can't make me."

She could. When our mother told us to do something, we did it. Other kids bragged about the spankings they got. We just said, "You should see our mother's Withering Look!"

As soon as supper was over, I was dispatched to my first C.G.I.T. meeting.

I did not know much about this group. I knew the letters stood for Canadian Girls In Training. They wore sailor middies with dark-blue skirts. They met once a week, and you had to be twelve to join. What they were in training for was a mystery.

I dawdled. The later I was, the less time I'd have to stand on the outskirts of another group that did not want me.

As I pulled open the big church door, I heard music. I slowly made my way down the stairs toward the sound. As I reached the large room where the group met, I saw, with horror, that they were dancing.

I could not dance. And I knew from experience that they would not be able to teach me. They would say things like, "Move this foot that way and then take two steps like this."

There are no harder words for a visually impaired person to fathom than "there," "here," "these," or "this." I stood still just inside the door, hoping nobody would see me.

"Jean, how lovely! You're just in time," said one of the kindest, warmest voices I had ever heard.

Marian Paton, the minister's daughter, was hurrying toward me with both hands outstretched.

"What?" I said inanely.

Marian laughed, a rich chuckle that set me more at ease than a paragraph of welcoming words could have done.

"We're an uneven number," she explained, drawing me into the line of laughing girls. She had to raise her voice to be heard above the music of the Virginia Reel. "I had to sit out because there was nobody to be my partner. Don't worry. I'll tell you exactly what to do."

She did, too. I understood every word she said. It wasn't hard. I copied what she did. We bowed to each other. We twirled around. We skipped forward and back.

I was having fun.

When the dance ended, she introduced me to everyone. The leaders, Miss Cowie and Marg, were as kind as she was.

We sat in a circle and sang songs. I loved singing. We had a short worship service. It was not boring and over my head. I liked it. Miss Cowie read a poem.

> Life has loveliness to sell,
> All beautiful and splendid things,
> Blue waves whitening on a cliff,
> Soaring fire that sways and sings,
> And children's faces looking up,
> Holding wonder like a cup.

I had written lots of poems by now. I loved this one. Miss Cowie went on reading the next verse. It ended:

> And, for your spirit's still delight,
> Holy thoughts that star the night.

I drew a deep breath and let it out in a sigh of bliss. This was the way to share poetry. At school, we had to take it apart. Long, short, long, short. Or decide it was iambic pentameter. Here poetry was to delight in, to listen to, to draw pictures with inside your head. I had seen Pat's face "looking up, holding wonder like a cup."

Then, in an incredibly short time, we were standing in a circle with crossed arms and linked hands, singing Taps.

I walked home alone. I didn't mind. It had been wonderful. I could hardly wait till next week. They had liked me. Nobody had said "cross-eyed" once. What was even nicer was that I felt nobody had even thought it.

It was dark, but I was not afraid. I looked up at the stars and smiled. I knew, in my head, that sighted people saw millions of them on a night like this, too many to count. I decided their sky must be cluttered. I leaned my head way back counting my measure of stars. Six. No, seven. I thought of the lines in the poem Miss Cowie had read.

> And, for your spirit's still delight,
> Holy thoughts that star the night.

I could write a poem about my seven stars.

Then, before I had even the first line done, I realized I was nearly home. Mother had not said so but I knew she would have been wondering how I was getting along.

I ran the last block, burst into the house and went straight to her office door. She opened it quickly, as though she had been listening for my knock.

"Jean, how was it?" she asked.

She began to smile before I could start to tell her. My face must have been shining as brightly as my seven stars.

❧ 18 ❧

Mr. Benham, the principal of Victory School and my eighth grade teacher, was special. He liked, really liked, every one of us. Boys who had given other teachers trouble settled down and worked in his class.

Mr. Benham even liked Rob.

I liked Rob, too, although I had never once talked with him. He was an outsider like me. Otherwise I might not have watched him the way I did. The difference between us was that I yearned to be liked, while Rob did not seem to care. He sat slouched in his desk, staring out the window, as if he were alone in the room.

He came from the country, and he skipped school every chance he got. There was a limit to how many times you could play hooky without getting the strap. Rob broke that limit every time the sun shone. I never heard him give an excuse, but somehow we all knew he stayed home to help his father on the farm. We knew, too, that Rob's dad thought school was a waste of time.

After he had been absent several days, the truant officer would go after him. When he hauled him into the principal's office, Mr. Benham would have to give him the strap.

One morning when Rob had been missing most of a week, I heard the dreaded knock on our classroom door. When Mr. Benham went into his next-door office, we could not help hearing the lecture Rob got, his total silence and then the sound of the leather strap striking his palm.

I wanted to cover my ears. Instead I dug my fingernails into my own palms and waited for it to be over. Rob did not so much as gasp.

The two of them came into the classroom. Mr. Benham's hand was on Rob's shoulder. Rob, a skinny, deeply tanned boy with a mop of uncombed black hair, stared straight ahead.

As I pretended not to be stealing sideways glances at him, I knew what Mr. Benham would do next. I waited to see if I had guessed correctly. Ten minutes passed.

"All right, class, put your books away," our teacher said. "It's time we had a lesson on agriculture."

I was right. Sometimes he called it nature study, sometimes agriculture. But always we studied it shortly after Rob was returned to the class. Next Mr. Benham would show us pictures of huge work horses with hairy feet or wildflowers or fields of grain.

"Who can tell me what this is?" he'd ask.

I would feel ignorant. Nobody else would know, either. Rob would glance at the picture and then go back to gazing out the window. Yet when Mr. Benham finally said, "Rob, can you tell them?" he would toss back the answer as if anybody would know that. "Barley," he would say, "Jack-in-the-pulpit" or "Clydesdale."

Today it was a close-up picture of a horse in harness.

"Who can name the different parts of a horse's harness?" Mr. Benham asked.

As he actually managed to get Rob up to the front to point out the various pieces, I decided Mr. Benham must have been a country boy himself. As he and Rob named off plants and animals and farm machinery, they seemed to share a kinship that excluded the rest of us.

Rob walked back to his seat, not looking to the left or right. Yet there was something about him that had changed. I did not say the word "pride" to myself, but I recognized it all the same.

I understood that Mr. Benham was having us study those things on purpose. Rob was unable to read one sentence without stumbling over at least two words. He could not spell. But he knew more about agriculture than anybody else. I felt clever to have seen what my teacher was doing for Rob.

I did not see that he was also teaching us that education does not come only from between the covers of books, but from the worlds outside the classroom door.

I learned other things that year.

We were studying part of a poem called "The Deserted Village" by Oliver Goldsmith. Mr. Benham read the lines aloud. He stopped at the words, "The swain responsive as the milkmaid sung."

"Who can tell us what 'swain' means?"

My hand shot up almost before the question was out of his mouth. I might lag behind in some subjects, but I was convinced I was the best student in the class when it came to English.

"Yes, Jean," Mr. Benham said. "What does 'swain' mean?"

"Pigs," I said triumphantly, extremely proud of myself and my amazing vocabulary.

"Pigs . . ." Mr. Benham echoed, staring at me for a split second, as though he had not heard me properly. Then my teacher, suddenly and without warning, went into a paroxysm of laughter. He roared. He slapped his knee with the book. He took a turn or two around. He had to remove his glasses to wipe away tears of mirth. Throughout the whole performance, he kept gasping out, "Pigs. She said Pigs!"

I stared at him totally bewildered. The class, who had no notion of what was so tickling him, nevertheless whooped with glee. Whatever the joke was, they enjoyed it to the full. They shrieked and they shook and they all looked at me. If I had known of a suitable method, I would cheerfully have killed every single one of them, teacher included.

Finally he got control of himself. He grinned at me.

"'Swine' means pigs, Jean," he explained. "'Swain' means sweetheart. It could well be that her swain was a swine, but we won't go into that."

Sweetheart! I blushed up to my ears. I longed to run away and never return. I pretended I did not care. I knew that everybody else knew that I was pretending.

At recess, I was sure I heard someone whisper, "Pigs!" And then someone snickered. I stalked off and talked to my tree. It, I felt, was far more civilized than my swinish classmates.

I had forgiven Mr. Benham by the time we disagreed over the Prodigal Son. He had read us the story from the Bible. Then he began to talk to us about the plight of this poor, foolish boy, spending his money on a great spree and then finding himself lonely and humiliated and in want.

"We all feel sorry for the Prodigal Son, don't we?" he finished. "You can't help but have a soft spot for him. How many like the Prodigal better than the Elder Brother?"

The class knew the answer he wanted. Every hand went up. Every hand but mine.

While Mr. Benham had been explaining the sad life of the Prodigal, I had been thinking about that poor Elder Brother. There he was, staying home, being good, and nobody thanked him. Then a calf was born. Its mother died and he raised it by hand. It followed him around like a pet. But he had work to do, so he left the calf in its pen and went out into the fields. After all, he had to work twice as hard to make up to his father for that younger brother's desertion. When he came back to the house at sunset, tired out and hungry, he stopped to pat the calf. It was not in its pen. He asked a nearby servant. "Oh, your father told me to roast the fatted calf," said the man, "and that one was the fattest. That brother of yours is home and he's having the calf for supper right this minute."

"Jean, you don't mean to tell me that you like the Elder Brother better?" my teacher's voice broke in on the heart-rending scene.

"Yes," I said. "He was better. He stayed home. He worked hard. He didn't waste his money in the city."

Mr. Benham tried to laugh off my hot defence of the surly Elder Brother. I glared up at the poor man, furious at him for making light of the hurt I was sure the older boy had suffered. My eyes and my teacher's met and held. I refused to look down or smile. His face reddened.

"Maybe you'd better stay in after four and we can talk it over then," he said, his voice a bit gruff.

It was not till then that I realized I had been shouting. That Elder Brother meant a lot to me. I took every spare moment throughout the day writing a poem about him. After four, I put the poem into

Mr. Benham's hands. He sat and read it. Then he looked up at me with an odd smile.

"I hadn't realized that bit about the calf," he said. "I see what you mean. Someday, Jean, you'll be a writer."

He took time to read lots of things to us. He knew we needed to hear words used well if we were ever to care about using them well ourselves. One morning he sat on the edge of his desk and began to read us a long, exciting poem called "The Lady of the Lake." As the suspense mounted, I sat forward, loving the ring of it, the danger, the flash and dazzle, the pictures of a people unlike ourselves. He read page after page. Then, just as he got to the beginning of the end, he closed the book. He looked over the class.

"You'll find it in every library," he said. "It's by Sir Walter Scott. If you want to know how it turns out, you'll have to go to the library."

I could not believe he meant it. He did.

I was too annoyed at him to go to the library right away. But after a few days, I went. I had read my way through most of the Children's Library by that time. Yet though I was now thirteen, I had not thought till then of venturing upstairs.

All on my own I climbed the long, curving flight of stone steps to the impressive front doors. Inside, I climbed more stairs and approached the high desk.

"Have you a book with a poem in it called 'The Lady of the Lake'?" I inquired in a small voice.

The stout lady sitting there gave me a long look. Then she nodded. She glanced pointedly at some tall file cabinets. Then she looked at my uncomprehending face again and sighed.

Was she going to send me back downstairs? I had

brought Mother's library card. Was that against the rules?

"Aren't you Llew Little's girl?" she demanded, her voice wheezing slightly.

It was my turn to nod. She smiled at me then. But she did not move. I waited. This librarian was older than Miss Metcalf. I knew about old people. They got tired. At last she tucked her pencil behind her ear.

"Follow me," she said and led the way to the poetry section. Her glance skimmed the titles. Then she pointed her finger unerringly at the very book I sought.

"Thank you," I murmured. I reached for the book. I frowned at the smallish print. Oh, well, I could manage it if I stayed near one of the tall windows. Before trying to find the poem, I automatically flipped to the back of the book. There was a blue card in the pocket!

I hesitated. I knew I hated blue card books. Yet I did want to find out what happened to Roderick Dhu. I checked the Contents page. There it was. The Lady of the Lake.

I sat down and read and read, my nose flattened against the glossy pages. At last I reached the end.

Giving a great sigh of satisfaction, I closed the fat volume of Scott's poems. I put it back in its place. I began idly examining other collections on nearby shelves. Why, there was a book of poems by Robert Louis Stevenson. I had imagined his one poetry book to have been *The Child's Garden of Verses*. I opened this other one at random.

> I will make you brooches and toys for your
>   delight
> Of birdsong at morning and starshine at night.

I will make a palace fit for you and me
Of green days in forests and blue days at
    sea . . .

And this shall be for music, when no-one else is
    near,
The fine song for singing, the rare song to hear!
That only I remember, that only you admire,
Of the broad road that stretches and the
    roadside fire.

I finished it in one delighted gulp and started again at the beginning. I went on to read another poem, oblivious of the world around me and the passing of time. Coming to myself as dusk began to fall, making the print impossible to decipher any longer, I went to the desk and checked out Stevenson's book of poems. I was hooked.

Mr. Benham had not just lured me into the Adult Library. He had taught me that all the good books did not have white cards in the back. There was a whole section of poetry here with a blue card in every book.

I wandered up and down those shelves for years, feasting on words. I discovered Edna St. Vincent Millay, then Emily Dickinson. At last, both the Brownings and John Keats. After that there was no stopping me.

As spring started to warm into summer, the newscasts began to predict the end of the war in Europe. Each day we would wait. Then, on the morning of May 8th, right in the middle of grammar, the whistles at the factories began to blow. Church bells chimed. A fire siren started.

We were on the edge of our seats.

"It's the end of the War," one girl yelled. "It's Peace."

Mr. Benham pointed his finger at us.

"You stay right where you are," he ordered, "until I check."

He ran into his office. As we waited, the noise outside the open windows got louder. Everybody was talking, some shouting. A couple whistled through their fingers. Then our teacher was back, a grin splitting his face. He waved his arms at us as if he were shooing away chickens.

"You can all go home!" he cried. "It's true. The war in Europe is over!"

❧ 19 ❧

I was at camp again when the war with Japan ended. We did not even know about it till the next day. It was the same private camp where I had been so miserable the year before. I was still an outsider, but I had a better time. I even passed a canoe test. I was a little less meek. C.G.I.T. had made me braver.

When camp ended, high school began. The first day in grade nine was bewildering. Up until then, I had had only one teacher each year. Now all at once I had nine. Also, most of my previous teachers had known about my poor vision before I arrived in their class. Now only my C.G.I.T. leader Miss Cowie, who had a grade ten homeroom, was aware of my special problems. And she was not even in the same building as I was.

The Guelph Collegiate Vocational Institute was housed in two buildings, the old school made of stone, and the new brick school. All the grade nine home rooms were in the old building; we had to scurry back and forth through rain and snow until a connecting corridor was added.

Confusing as it was, I survived that day. We had no classes, just trekked from room to room, learning our timetables and the names of texts. I went to bed that night tired and tense but thinking I might be able to manage.

The terrible moment came on the second day when I had my first home economics class.

"I will show you once where everything goes.

After that, you are to remember," Miss Cray told us sternly.

She went through a rapid inventory of the room. Here were the dishes, here the sugar, here the flour, here the dish towels and so on. She sounded fierce, so everybody watched and remembered except me. I could not see where she was pointing.

We cooked tea biscuits in the first class. Mine were as hard as rocks. We ate them anyway. They didn't taste remotely like Mother's or Grandma's. Then we cleaned up the mess.

"Where do you put the tea towel?" I asked somebody.

Had Miss Cray been waiting for me to ask? If not, she certainly pounced with astonishing speed.

"What did you say?" she demanded. She sounded angry.

I was not particularly worried. I knew I had a good reason for not knowing.

"I asked where the tea towels go. I couldn't see when you were showing us," I told her. I felt self-conscious but not afraid. "I have bad eyes," I added nervously.

It was as though I had touched off a short fuse. Miss Cray exploded.

"You should be in an institution. I'm paid to teach normal students; not abnormal ones. I can't be expected to change my teaching for somebody like you. Your parents should know enough not to send you here. You don't belong in a regular school. You belong in Brantford."

The bell signalling the end of the class broke into her tirade. She had to stop. When silence fell again, she just stood there, flushed and short of breath. The girls around me began gathering up their books. I tore my eyes away from her face and looked at them. I caught glances of secret sympathy. One girl took the tea towel from my nerveless hand and put it in its right place. I could not thank her. I could not have spoken if I had been offered money to do so. I picked up my books and my zippered case, balanced them on my left hip and forced myself to turn and look at the teacher. Was she through with me? Could I go?

She was staring down at something on the floor. I glanced down and saw a white speck, probably a bit of dough. She was standing very close to me. As she bent, with a cluck of her tongue, to pick it up, I noticed what a straight, pink parting she had in her hair. It wasn't pretty hair. I was obscurely comforted.

On Christmas Day the year I turned 16.

Chin up, I marched out of her room. I had made a vow. I was never, ever going to set foot in her classroom again. She wouldn't have to teach me. Nobody at that school would have to teach me.

I waited out the afternoon. Then I went home and was free to cry the way I had yearned to ever since Miss Cray had spoken to me in that harsh, despising tone. I faced my parents, tears streaming down my cheeks.

"I won't go back there," I told them defiantly. "If I have to be educated, I'll have tutors at home. I've read books about children having tutors. You can't make me go back because I won't go, no matter what you say."

Mother and Dad looked at each other. They said nothing at all for a long painful moment. I knew that they were deeply disturbed, angry and hurt by what I had told them. Neither of them tried to tell me I had exaggerated the whole thing or suggested that it was not worth bothering about.

But they did not call their lawyer, either. Nor did they rush to make an appointment with the principal or call the chairman of the school board.

"Do you have a home economics class tomorrow?" Mother asked at last.

I shook my head.

"But I'm not going back. Maybe she's not the only one who thinks that way. Maybe . . ."

Dad interrupted me, his sober, quiet tone contrasting with my passionate outburst.

"Jean, what has happened to you should certainly not have happened," he said. "But before we do anything impulsively, let's try thinking. You say you can be tutored. If it comes to that, I am sure we can arrange it. But sitting in this house with a tutor, you will have no friends your own age. You don't just learn history and French at school; you learn how to get along with people. Think what a triumph it would be if you could show Miss Cray how wrong she is."

I went on crying, but more quietly. I wanted to give up. I felt such a powerful yearning to retreat from the unending battle to be like everyone else, to sit in my pleasant, familiar home with a personal tutor and never have to struggle to belong again.

The few seconds I had stood, transfixed, listening to Miss Cray's blighting words had not been the only difficult moment in my first day. It had all been hard. Where to sit, what to do about invisible but important things written on the board, how to be sure teachers and other students were speaking to me when I could not see them, how to recognize my new classmates, how to tell an acute accent from a grave one in my French text when all I saw was a tiny grey smudge. All of these and a host of other small and large problems had confronted me.

Worst of all, perhaps, was the knowledge that any second some unexpected but even more threatening difficulty might present itself. I was tensed to meet such a challenge most of the time. Even in English class, where I knew all the answers, I was not sure there would not be something sprung on me. And what if I could not handle it?

I had attended only one day of classes and I felt worn out. I did not want to face another such day.

"Leave us to talk it over, Jean," my mother told me gently. "Perhaps Miss Cowie could help. Go read a book."

Mother knew what I needed. I went to my room,

wept a little longer, dozed briefly and then escaped into Frances Hodgson Burnett's *A Little Princess*.

Miss Minchin was so much worse than Miss Cray and yet Sara Crewe, without once stooping to unworthy tactics, defeated her completely. It did not matter a whit that Sara was years younger than I. I had had all the teenagers I could bear.

Miss Cowie went to see Miss Cray. Mother and Dad persuaded me to give high school another chance.

"Try it for a couple of weeks," they said. "If it doesn't get easier, we'll think some more."

It did get easier. I soon knew my way around both the old school and the new. Miss Cray pretended I was not there. When I could not see something, one of the other girls helped without my having to ask. Although none of them was the kindred spirit I still longed to find, I began to realize that I did have friends.

The work was harder for me to master now. I began to fail in algebra, in French, in geography. But with much coaching at home, I managed to pass into grade ten.

Miss Cowie not only became my homeroom teacher, she taught me English literature and composition. I loved that because she asked harder, more interesting questions and because she really liked poetry. She even liked my poetry. I would linger at the end of class to hand her something I had written, and she always looked delighted. I felt myself growing taller in the warmth of her approval.

In home economics, though, I had a new problem. This year we were supposed to learn to sew. Miss Freeman, our teacher, was kindness itself, but since I could not see well enough to sew, she made me knit.

"Blind people are wonderful knitters," she told me.
Some blind people undoubtedly were. I was not.

Miss Freeman began each class period by casting on a row of stitches for me to knit. I would sit there, knitting doggedly away at a flat, dull strip, until the bell rang and the period was over. I always dropped several stitches. Miss Freeman would look at the oblong of crooked rows filled with unsightly holes and shake her head. Then she would rip it out, and start the next class by casting on a new row so that I could begin the joyless task all over again.

"I don't want to knit. I'm not getting any better. Couldn't I read instead?" I pleaded, showing her an enormous copy of *Les Miserables* which I was longing to go on with.

"This is a home economics class," Miss Freeman reminded me patiently. "Reading novels is not home economics."

Then one day at the start of a double period lasting ninety minutes, Miss Freeman only cast on one stitch for me before she was called away. I did not wait by her desk for her to return. I took the single stitch to an out-of-the-way corner and began to knit it. I knit it off one needle onto the other, and then off the second needle back onto the first.

The girls around me watched, fascinated, as a long skinny chain began to stretch down from my busy needles. After Miss Freeman returned, they bunched around me whenever she glanced in our direction, keeping me hidden from her gaze. Nobody said anything. Everyone was waiting.

At the close of sewing class, Miss Freeman would get each girl to hold up what she had accomplished. I was working toward that moment. For nearly ninety minutes I had knitted on my chain. It was long, impressive and utterly useless.

"All right, girls," our teacher said, as I had hoped she would, "let's all see what has been done today."

One by one the girls rose and showed what stage they had reached in the sewing project. Then, as my turn came, Miss Freeman looked conscience-stricken.

"Oh, Jean, I'm sorry," she said. "I didn't cast on your stitches . . ."

Before she could say another word, I got to my feet and held up my long thin string of knitting.

"Yes, you did," I said. "This is what I've accomplished."

The girls around me tried to smother their laughter.

Miss Freeman stared at what I was holding up. Our eyes met. I did not need to say another word.

"Next Home Ec. period," my teacher said slowly, "you may bring your book."

As I opened *Les Miserables* the following week, some of my classmates muttered about Teacher's Pets getting out of sewing. But there I sat, my snub nose pressed close to the small print, utterly content and openly different. Reading was worth being different for. Little by little, I was sorting out when and whether belonging really mattered. Little by little, I was choosing to be me. Little by little, I was discovering what brought me joy and learning its price.

☙ 20 ☙

"I'm having a necking party on Friday night," Laurie announced airily as we walked home from school one day. "My mum's going to be out. You can bring any boy you like."

I had friends at last. I walked to school and home again, most days, with Laurie, June and Beth. Laurie was the star of the foursome. She was pretty and popular. Like my childhood friend Marilyn Dickson, she had naturally curly hair. She also had boyfriends. Beth, June and I were all proud to be her friends, and each of us longed to be her *best* friend.

In my secret heart, I could not understand why she bothered with me. After all, I was still cross-eyed. I was becoming overweight. It never crossed my mind that Laurie might like having me around because I admired her so much and was absolutely no threat. I was so grateful to her for allowing me to become one of her satellites that I would have done anything to please her.

That is what I thought until she invited me to her necking party.

When she smiled and waited for our reaction, June and Beth giggled and twittered excitedly. How they really felt I had no idea.

I felt appalled. But I did my best to appear cool, casual, a woman of the world.

"I'm really sorry but I can't come," I said with an exaggerated sigh of disappointment. "My mother has something going on that night and I have to stay home."

They exchanged amused glances. My face burned but I stuck to my lame excuse. After all, they had no proof that I was lying.

I underestimated Laurie.

"I'll walk you home," she said. When we reached my house, she waited around until my mother came out of the office.

"I'm really disappointed that Jean can't come to my party on Friday night," she said sadly.

Mother was startled. She looked at me.

"Why can't you go?" she asked.

I stuttered something about thinking I had too much homework.

Mother, wanting to help me make friends, said, "But you'll have all day Saturday. Surely you can do your homework then. I think you should go."

Laurie smiled like a cat who had polished off a quart of whipping cream. When we were outside, she said, "I'll ask a boy for you, don't worry. It'll be a great party."

She had outmanoeuvred me so smoothly that I was trapped. I could think of no other way to escape. If I explained to Mother, she might want me to stop being friends with Laurie. I couldn't do that. I had no other friends.

I worried about that party so much that I could not sleep at night. I felt sure the others were laughing at me behind my back. I knew that if I did go, I would have no idea how to behave. If Laurie really did ask a boy for me, I was positive that when he found out who his date was to be, he would be furious. What if she invited a boy who was as great a social misfit as I was? I knew she was quite capable of doing exactly that and waiting to laugh at the result.

On Friday morning I was three blocks away from the collegiate when I slipped on a bit of ice and fell. I landed with my left leg doubled back under me. The pain was intense. I knew even before I tried to get up that I was really hurt.

I would not be able to go to Laurie's party!

My relief was so great that I bore the pain with fortitude. The drama of the thing helped, too. I was much closer to school than I was to our house. What an entrance I was going to make!

It took me half an hour to hobble the three short blocks. I stepped forward a baby step with my uninjured foot and then dragged the lame one after it. I arrived as my classmates were coming out of our homeroom.

"You're late," Laurie cried at the sight of me.

"I couldn't help it," I ground out. "I think I've broken my leg."

"Jean, you have cracked your ankle bone," Mother said when they got the results of the X-ray. "It's a shame. I'm afraid you won't be able to go to that party."

"It doesn't matter," I said in a brave voice. "How long do I have to stay in bed?"

I had to stay there for several weeks. Mother kept telling me what a perfect patient I was.

"You are taking it so well," she marvelled.

I did not explain why I was so cheerful.

I had a lovely time. Mother brought me stacks of library books. They let me have extras because I was an invalid. I scribbled down flowery poems and romantic prose bits. I showed them to my father. He read them and frowned.

"Write about what you know," he told me. "You can do better than this. You write too much about sunsets and pixies."

Furious at him, I wrote a story about a little girl called Elizabeth who believed in fairies. Her callous father jeered at her. "You are ridiculous," he scoffed. Elizabeth gazed at him with huge, sad eyes and went out to chat with an elf.

I thought the story showed my father how curmudgeonly and unimaginative he was. Yet I could not help noticing that I myself found Elizabeth and her father far more interesting to write about than that elf. Without telling Dad, I gave up pixies.

After a day or two, I put my typewriter on the bed table and wrote my first longish story about real people. It took the shape of a fifteen-year-old girl's diary. She had an older sister, twin younger brothers, perfect parents and a strait-laced great-aunt who lived with them and tried to make the children behave like little ladies and gentlemen. Even though it was a story about a girl named Mary Kentworth, lots of me slipped in. Mary was excited about Christmas coming; she wrote poems; she lived in a large stone house; she found the old lady who shared their home crabby; she went into raptures over their new puppy and she enjoyed choosing presents for the people she loved.

She was also addicted to phrases like "tattered blue woodsmoke." I had learned, from reading and rereading L. M. Montgomery's books, a lot about making the feelings of children come through, but I had also learned to rhapsodize about nature. Mary could not delete sunsets, either.

Dad was pleased that I had stopped writing coyly about elves. He liked Mary Kentworth much better.

But now he had new advice.

"Put conflict in, Jean. You cannot have a plot without conflict."

"But what if my characters just don't *have* any conflict?" I asked, scowling at him. "What if they are perfectly happy people?"

"There isn't any such animal," my father said. "Not one worth writing a book about, anyway. They'd come out like tapioca puddings."

I laughed. He had not convinced me, but I would remember.

When I returned to school, I found other friends, the kind I had always dreamed of having. Grace and Barbara and Norma and I would talk for hours. At last I stood on street corners, unable to part from girls I'd spent the day with. And after supper we would have to phone each other to exchange our smallest, most trivial thoughts.

In summer, I went to Miramichi, a C.G.I.T. camp, and discovered, much to my surprise, that I loved camping after all. The whole atmosphere was so different from that of the private camp I had attended. Grace, Barbara and Norma were there, too.

Even at camp, though, I still often felt lonely and left out. I worried over what people thought of me. I admired some counsellors extravagantly, placing them on sky-high pedestals. When they teetered a little, I steadied them.

One of these crushes turned into a lifelong friendship. Elizabeth Kerr encouraged me in my writing even after camp was over. She wrote to me once telling me that my letters and poems lifted her "out of the mundane into the world of things that count." I had to look up mundane in the dictionary, but once I understood what she meant, I held onto that sentence like a lucky charm, repeating it to myself whenever I needed its balm.

I was afraid my new friends would someday realize that I was the cross-eyed, show-off, crybaby, tattletale Teacher's Pet I had been called all those years. I kept needing to be reassured.

Sometimes, when I was feeling particularly insecure, I would trip over a stone or run into a tree deliberately. Everyone would be apologetic. "Don't worry," I would say. "I'm fine." I was ashamed of myself every time. Yet I did it again.

We moved to an even more gigantic, delightful house when I was fourteen. My room was on the third floor. It had a slanting ceiling, a skylight and a casement window. Even though it was a long climb up two flights of stairs, I loved it. It seemed to come right out of a book.

When my bedtime arrived on my fifteenth birthday, I was sitting in the den rereading *Jane Eyre* for the fourth time. Jamie, home for Christmas from St. Andrew's College, was out at a party. Grandma had gone up to her room and Hugh and Pat had already been sent to bed. Mum and Dad, also absorbed in reading, sat across from me.

As the hands of the mantel clock inched toward ten, Jane was out in the dark lane, about to be nearly run down by Rochester's horse. I could not bear to be interrupted. I scrunched low in my chair and endeavoured to become invisible. If only I could escape my parents' notice for another ten minutes, I could enjoy the whole thrilling encounter.

I finished the chapter and stole a look at my watch.

It was twenty past ten! I could not believe my luck. Hardly breathing, I started on the next chapter.

I finished it, too! Surely, any second now, Mum would catch sight of the time and sweep me upstairs. After all, even though Jamie still had some holidays left, I had to go back to school in the morning. Surreptitiously, I once more checked my watch. It was five to eleven. I could not remember ever having been up so late on a school night.

Then Mother yawned. She closed her book and rose. She did not look at me. Dad got up, carrying his book with him, and went out to the hall. Mother turned to leave the room, but at the door, she glanced back.

"You'll turn the lights out before you come up, won't you?" she said lightly.

My mouth dropped open. I stared at her. Then I squeaked, "It's way past my bedtime. You forgot to send me to bed."

"You are fifteen," my mother told me. "You should have sense enough by now to go to bed at a reasonable hour. From now on, your bedtime is your responsibility. Good night."

Dad was waiting for her at the foot of the stairs. As she joined him, I heard the two of them laughing.

They had known the time all along. They were laughing at me. I felt intensely annoyed. Then I looked down at my open book. I could stay up all night, if I liked, and finish it. The freedom dazzled me.

Then, in spite of myself, I was overtaken by an enormous yawn. I grinned, got up, turned off the lights and followed my parents up the stairs to bed.

The following Christmas, my father gathered up the poems I had been writing since I was eleven and looked them over.

"I think we should have these printed," he told Mother and me. "There are enough for a nice little book which we could give our friends. I think we could even sell some."

Mother looked doubtful. I was ecstatic.

He came in the next day smiling broadly.

"I asked Evan if he'd illustrate the poems," he said, "and he has agreed to do it."

Mother shook her head at his effrontery. Evan Macdonald was a Guelph artist who painted portraits and landscapes. Why on earth would he want to illustrate a teenager's poems? But Dad got his way as usual. The tiny pictures greatly enhanced the book.

From beginning to end, Dad was in complete charge. He went through the poems, improving on the metre here and there, asking me to rewrite sometimes, not listening when our opinions differed, adding words and phrases of his own. I have never had a tougher editor. It was a fine preparation for working with "real" editors later.

He named the booklet "It's a Wonderful World."

When he put the finished slim volume into my hands, I leafed through it. For the first time I saw my words actually in print. I caught my breath. They looked so much more special, somehow, so convincing and important.

I stopped flipping through the pages, beaming idiotically, and paused long enough to read the perfect poems. The fact that they were printed had given them a little extra polish, but to my chagrin, they were not perfect after all. Here and there, one of my own cherished verses read awkwardly. Most of Dad's changes jarred. He had ruined some of my best lines.

I opened my mouth to tell him so. Then I subsided, the words unspoken. If it were not for his love of my work, there would not be any slim, almost perfect book. And he positively glowed with pride in me.

I returned to the title page where he had put a small oval picture of me looking ethereal. Something was written under the picture. I peered at it.

"Why does it just say 1932 - ?" I asked. "It should say 1932 - 1947."

"No," my father said. "It would only say that if you were dead. You are still alive. This is only your first book. And I wanted people to know that you are still just fifteen."

"Nearly sixteen," I reminded him.

But I liked what he had said. "This is only your first book."

DECEMBER TWILIGHT

Orange clouds were drifting
No overhanging grey
Dimmed the rosy sunset,
At the close of day.

Royal purple nestled
Round a golden cloud,
Leafless, wind-blown poplars
Before their Maker bowed.

O'er the snowy landscape
Christmas chimes rang out,
While in neighboring door-ways,
Happy children shout.

Many busy people, late,
Their tiresome work took leave
To hurry home and welcome
This year's Christmas eve.

The title page of my first book, and "December Twilight"
(*I still like "Orange flags were flying" better.*)

❧ 21 ❧

"This is it, Jeanie," Belle said, steering me toward the doors of the Royal Alexandra Theatre.

I had been hunched up, trying to fend off the biting wind of the bleak January afternoon, but I scarcely noticed when we left it behind. I was too busy staring around at the people, listening to tantalizing fragments of conversation, catching the expectancy that made the lobby feel festive and friendly. There were quite a few kids. I was not the only one who had been given a ticket to *A Midsummer Night's Dream* that Christmas.

This was my first chance to see a Shakespearean play performed live, by real actors and actresses in a proper theatre. And Belle had not brought anybody but me.

She handed our tickets to the usher.

"Front row centre seats!" he said with approval.

I felt a momentary pang of guilt as Belle sent me a conspiratorial grin. I had so often been jealous of the special treats she seemed to lavish on Hugh and Pat. For years I had been certain she liked them far better than she liked me.

"You would be a much happier girl if you stopped stewing over what other people think about you," Mother frequently pointed out.

Realizing that I was wasting my precious evening doing exactly that, I stopped and followed Belle and the usher down the richly carpeted aisle to our seats. I glimpsed people already seated in the rows we passed. I felt their eyes on us. It was as though I were an actress playing the part of a girl walking down a theatre aisle. I sat down and shrugged out of my coat as if I were somebody famous. I presented Belle with the kind of smile I thought June Allyson or Elizabeth Taylor would have worn at such a moment.

She gave me a genuine Belle Dauphinee grin in return.

Belle was a friend of Mother's who had become a friend to all of us while Dad was overseas. Though Mother was only an inch over five feet in height, she towered over Belle. But what Belle lacked in inches, she made up for in merriment and vitality. She played games with us and planned special occasions like this trip to the matinee at the Royal Alex.

"It's nearly curtain time," she said. "Are you excited?"

I nodded. The musicians in the orchestra pit below us now tuned their instruments and began to play. I wanted to part the red velvet curtains just in front of my knees and look down at them, but I did not. Pat would have done it, but she was a child of nine. I was fifteen.

The house lights dimmed. I stared at the curtain, determined not to miss seeing it go up. There! It rose magnificently. The stage was revealed. Theseus spoke.

> Now, fair Hippolyta, our nuptial hour draws on apace.
> Four happy days bring in another moon.

I gave a sigh of pure delight, eased off my left shoe which had been pinching my toes, and prepared to enjoy myself.

It was a charmed day. I loved the poetry, the costumes, the fairies Cobweb and Mustard Seed. As I watched them, I thought of Noel Streatfeild's novel, *Ballet Shoes*. Pauline and Petrova Fossil had played these very parts. Knowing something of the discipline necessary to play the roles added to their magic.

I was laughing at Bottom's antics when the dreadful thing happened. I had totally forgotten about the curtain, which was all that separated us from the orchestra. In my enthusiasm, I stretched out my left foot and kicked my shoe into the orchestra pit.

I squeaked with alarm.

"What's wrong?" Belle asked.

"My shoe! I've lost my shoe."

Belle laughed. I was mortified. I'd just leave it. Then I pictured myself going up the aisle with one shoe off and one shoe on. Scarlet with embarrassment and helpless with a fit of giggles, I got down on my knees, parted the curtain, poked my head through and gazed down at the players. They were grinning. Without a word, the first violinist handed my shoe back to me.

I put it firmly on my foot. Pinched toes or not, I was not going to let it escape me a second time.

I loved the play. I clapped till my palms stung. Then I turned to tell Belle how wonderful it had been. I was halfway through my speech of thanks when I heard our names. We were being paged!

"We have a telephone message for a Miss Belle Dauphinee and a Miss Jean Little," a voice announced. "Would Miss Dauphinee or Miss Little please come to the office before leaving the theatre."

Belle and I stared at each other, startled and

disbelieving.

"Who knows we're here?" I asked.

Belle got to her feet very suddenly. She began pushing her way through the crowd. I snatched up my coat and followed. I had thought the excitement was over, and here it was back again. I felt more like a person in a play than ever.

"We were asked to tell you that a Dr. Little wishes you to go to the Western Hospital on your way home," the manager told us.

Belle reared back and stared up into his face. She seemed unduly alarmed. My parents were doctors, after all, and they were always going to hospitals. Dad was in Ottawa. Perhaps he had come this far and wanted a ride to Guelph.

"Which Dr. Little?" Belle demanded.

The manager looked confused. He shook his head.

"I've told you the message as it was given to me. That is all I know."

"Dad must be there wanting a ride," I said.

Belle started for the door. She was not her usual chatty, laughing self. I still was not disturbed. I limped along, trying to keep up to her small, determined figure. I wished she would slow down. I was sure I was getting a blister on the little toe of my left foot.

Outside the theatre, darkness had fallen. Once in the car, I began to babble. I thanked her for taking me to the play. I told her the parts I liked best. I moaned about my embarrassment over having to retrieve my shoe. She laughed, but abstractedly, her attention on the traffic. I searched her face in the lights from passing cars. It seemed tense.

"I'm sure it's just Dad wanting a ride," I said again.

"How would he know we were at the play?" she

demanded, her voice sharp. I stopped trying to calm her down. Everything would be explained when we reached the hospital.

But when we went up to the front desk, they would not give us any information. It was puzzling. Although there seemed to be no message left for us, they definitely wished us to stay.

"But if Dr. Little isn't here, there's no point," Belle said.

"If you'll just sit down and wait, I'll see if I can find Dr. Little," the woman at the desk said blandly. "Take a seat, please."

We sat down. I relaxed. Belle sat at the edge of her chair. We waited. Time crawled by. I yawned and wished my father would hurry up. It was past suppertime.

Finally Belle could not wait another minute. She marched up to the desk and stood ready to give battle. I skulked nearby, embarrassed by her indignation.

"What is going on?" she said. "Is Dr. Little here or isn't she? Has something happened?"

"If you'll just wait, I'll see if they are ready," the woman snapped and went back to her switchboard. I moved to stand beside Belle. What did the lady mean by "they?" For the first time, I realized that this was not a normal happening. I felt suddenly very cold. My hands shoved themselves into my coat pockets and balled into tight fists.

Even though she kept her voice low, we both caught the tail end of her next words. " . . . accident ready yet?" I clutched Belle's arm. We held our breath.

"I'll send these people up then," we heard her say.

"Where . . .?" Belle began.

"If you will go to Emergency," the lady said, as

coolly as though she were telling us where to find the lingerie department, "you will find Dr. Little. They are prepared for you now."

My throat felt dry and tight. I gripped Belle's elbow, bulky in her winter coat. We got on the elevator. My knees started to shake.

The elevator doors parted. We stepped out into a wide hallway smelling of disinfectant and anaesthetic. And, walking down the hall toward us, with two purses on her arm, was my little sister.

"Patsy!" we cried. "What are you doing here? What happened?"

"We were in a car crash," Pat said proudly.

"Mum?" I croaked. Belle tensed beside me.

As we waited, I realized for the first time that my mother was mortal.

"She's alive but she's hurt," Pat said. "I haven't seen her yet but I saw her sitting up in the ambulance. I don't know about Grandma. They wouldn't let me look. A lady took me into her house and tried to make me drink some tea and take an aspirin. I said I hated tea and my sister was the one who took pills. I landed on my head in a snowbank. Feel the bump. It's huge!"

I stretched out my hand obediently to feel the impressive goose egg under her hair. I also began to breathe again. Mother was alive.

"When I got up, I saw their purses lying in the snow." Pat was talking too fast. "So I picked them up. They tried to take them away, but I'm keeping them till I see Mummy."

Her high voice wavered. I remembered that she was only nine and bent to hug her. We clung to each other till we heard Belle.

"Flora!" she cried. "Here she is, Jeanie. Oh, my

dear, you look as though you've been through a war."

Pat and I spun around. Mother was seated in a wheelchair. The moment she saw us, she made the orderly stop pushing it. Despite his protests, she started struggling to her feet. Pat did not wait. She flung herself at Mother, who sat back and caught her plus the two purses.

While she kissed my sister, I stared at her, trying to assess her injuries. Although later I saw that her face was scraped and bruised, her clothes stained and her coat minus a button, I saw none of these details at first. But I did see that she was not wearing her glasses. As I, too, leaned to kiss her, I also saw she looked exhausted.

Her voice, when it came, was unsteady but reassuringly her own.

"You got my message then," she said. "Poor Mother has taken the brunt of it. I'm all right. But the car is done for, I'm afraid. I'll have to settle about leaving Mother here. Then we can go. It's time Pat was home in bed."

Belle tried to persuade her to stay in the hospital till the next day, at least.

"Rubbish," Mother scoffed. "I'm fine. I just have to talk to them about Mother. Oh, here she comes."

She sounded so normal that I had been momentarily reassured. It shocked me to see two nurses wheeling Grandma toward us on a bed. They paused next to us. Mother got out of the wheelchair without a backward look and spoke gently to my grandmother.

"How goes it, Mother?" she asked.

Grandma made a gallant attempt to smile. I went to her other side. She reached out her sound hand and took hold of mine. She squeezed it. She did not speak.

"Go with her, Jeanie," Mother told me. "Don't let her talk too much. She needs rest. Take Pat along. We'll come in a few minutes."

We followed the nurses into a room. They fussed around Grandma's bed for a couple of minutes and then left. When Pat and I were alone with her, Grandma told us she was dying. I had enough of Mother in me to tell her that she was doing nothing of the sort. I hoped I was right. Grandma ignored this.

"Say 'The Lord is my shepherd' for me," she said. When I hesitated, she began to repeat the familiar words herself in a quavering voice.

"'He shall make me lie down in green pastures,'" I joined in, struggling to stop my own voice from shaking.

Grandma went on murmuring bits of the words and Pat came in for a phrase here and there. But I was left to carry the main part. It was a much harder part than Cobweb's or Mustard Seed's. As I reached, "Yea, though I walk through the valley of the shadow of death ..." I faltered. Grandma squeezed my hand again. My throat ached.

"'I will fear no evil,'" my little sister said in a strong, sure voice. I was aware that it was only because she knew that bit, but I was grateful for her steadiness. As we finished together, I realized that the end of the psalm was not about dying but about living. I was relieved. I was comforted, too, by the old, old words.

Grandma had a gash across her forehead that had required seventeen stitches, and her shoulder was broken. But she did not die for another thirteen years.

When we went out to the car, Pat sat beside Belle in the front. Mother lay in the back with her head on my lap. Belle drove very slowly. It was a bitterly cold night. My feet soon grew numb, but I would not have stirred for anything. Mother lay there covered with a blanket, not moving. I felt her weight with a gratitude that surpassed any emotion I had felt previously. By the time we got to Guelph, I had no sensation in my legs at all. I did not mind. It seemed a small thing next to the joy of serving my mother in such a direct way.

I did not think about myself. I did not think about Shakespeare. I did not remember that I had had no supper. I thought about the 23rd Psalm and Grandma in the hospital. I thought about Mother being safe, and tears of relief and tiredness and joy slipped down my ice-cold cheeks to dampen my coat collar.

✴ 22 ✴

When I was seventeen, I wrote two Christmas poems about Joseph and Mary's thoughts as they approached Bethlehem. As I sat writing, I felt I really was inside the hearts of this young couple who so long ago had made a difficult journey to an unfit shelter grudgingly given.

The poems made Mother cry. They made Dad excited. He submitted them to the weekly magazine, *Saturday Night*.

Under his prodding, I had started to keep a diary. I wrote in it spasmodically. Dad was always after me to date poems and diary entries, but I could see no sense in that. One entry is headed casually "Some day or other." Another reads "Thursday maybe." But one page has a definite date.

Wednesday, Nov. 22

This date should stay forever blazoned in my memory. Today I got a letter of acceptance from Toronto Saturday Night. They are going to publish "Mary" and "Joseph" in the Christmas issue. I practically lifted the roof off when I heard. Rose [the Dutch girl who worked for us] got knocked flat on the floor when I hugged her. Daddy asked her after if she was hurt and she said, "Oh No! Jean is happy. It did not hurt me. I think she has no headache now."

There was still a month to go before the poems

would be published. I thought the waiting might finish me off. But early in December I went into Toronto General Hospital to have my nose repaired. I had broken it when I was twelve and ran slam into a tree during a game of Hide and Seek. It had healed crookedly, blocking my breathing. Since this had resulted in frequent sore throats, I had to have an operation to unblock it.

I was lying in the big bed in the spare room, with a fire blazing comfortably in the fireplace, recuperating from my surgery when ten-year-old Pat came dashing in, waving the December 26th issue of *Saturday Night* as if it were a banner.

"They're in it," she shrieked, dancing up and down with excitement. "Your poems! They have a whole page!"

I snatched it from her and, as the magazine changed hands, lost the place. I fumbled through it, searching.

Dad and Mother arrived in the doorway.

"Here. Let me," my father said.

"No. There it is!" my sister cried, pushing his hand away. "She's got it."

I stared at the page. The poems were printed with black type on a white background. They were framed by a picture, drawn in white lines on a black background. Right beside the poems walked Joseph leading the donkey on which Mary rode. Underneath were a cow, a sheep and an angel in front of the Bethlehem Inn. At the top were a scatter of village houses, a palm tree and six stars.

My kind of sky, I thought dizzily.

Then I tried to read the words. My eyes misted and I could not see one of them. Dad reached out and took the magazine. He sat down beside me on the bed. Holding it so that I could still see the page, he read the poems aloud.

My father knew what was important. He had wanted to be a writer himself.

I listened. When he reached the lines,

It's been too long a way, too hard a fight.
I cannot bear your Saviour of the World
Tonight.

and his voice broke, I knew why I wanted to be a writer.

I took the magazine back and stared, eyes clear now, at my name.

Jean Little.

Dad got up and glanced out the window. It was dark. But it was not quite six o'clock.

"I'm going downtown to see if I can find some more copies," he said.

"Llew, supper's just ready," Mother called after him.

But he was gone. He and I were too excited to eat.

The publication of the poems made a sensation among my teachers and even impressed my classmates. Early in January, when I came home for lunch, I found a letter for me on the hall table. I carried it into the living room where the light was better. From there I could glimpse Dad still standing in the hall, reading his mail.

The envelope was from *Saturday Night*. I tore it open and stared at the slip of paper that fell into my hand. I had never had anything like it before. It said $30.00. I could make that out.

"Dad," I said uncertainly, "I think *Saturday Night* has sent me a bill for thirty dollars."

He came and looked over my shoulder. Then he grinned.

"It's not a bill. It's a cheque. They are paying you for the poems."

I stared from him to the cheque and back again. I would gladly have paid *Saturday Night* for the delight they had given me. It had not crossed my mind that they would pay me.

"You mean, it's mine? Thirty dollars?" I said, sounding dazed.

"You wrote the poems, didn't you?" my father said, laughing at my look of stupefaction. "You are a writer, Jean. Writers get paid for their work."

Work! It hadn't been work. It had been something I did for the love of doing it.

Thirty dollars! I wrote in my diary:

> I got the shock of my life in a cheque for $30.00 (thirty dollars) from Saturday Night. I really feel professional at last. I sent them another poem immediately, mercenary creature that I am.

The poem was turned down with a kind letter from B. K. Sandwell himself. I was disappointed, but not surprised. I knew in my heart of hearts that I had a lot to learn yet.

When I arrived at school one January morning, Miss Sinclair, my Latin teacher, met me in the hall.

"Jean, did you know there's a letter asking about you in the Letters to the Editor column in *Saturday Night*?"

"No!" I said, thrilled to the core to hear from my

admiring public.

We went to the library and there was the letter.

January 23, 1951

Thank you for those two finely sensitive poems, Mary and Joseph, published in the Dec. 25 issue. I hope the author is a Canadian.

J. A. Alexander
Toronto, Ont.

Beneath the letter, the Editors had replied: "Yes, she is a Canadian, living in Guelph, Ont."

I beamed at Miss Sinclair. She smiled mistily back at me.

"That's quite a compliment, Jean. You've done well," she said. Then she cleared her throat.

All morning, teachers stopped me in the hall to congratulate me. Even Mr. Hamilton, the principal, sought me out.

"This will be a proud day for your father," he said.

I felt like a celebrity. Much as I enjoyed the attention, however, I yearned to race home to show my family the letter. Instead I had to wait until noon. When at last I was free, I positively flew the mile and a half to our house. I burst into the dining room where the family was assembling for lunch. When I came to a halt, I gasped out, "Mum, somebody wrote to *Saturday Night* asking about me. Some man named J. A. Alexander. He liked my poems."

Mother did not say a word to me. Instead she sent a searching look down the table to where my father sat.

"Llew, you didn't!" she exclaimed.

I did not understand. What had Dad to do with

some strange man from Toronto? My puzzled gaze followed her accusing one. Dad was grinning. And blushing!

"Well, I just . . ." he began to defend himself.

At last the meaning of my mother's question registered. J. A. Alexander was my father.

I wanted to kill him. He had made me a laughing stock. If anybody found out that my own father had written that letter, I'd never live it down. Humiliated and speechless with rage, I sank into a chair.

He was proud of himself. He had signed the letter with an alias, and he had driven to Toronto to mail it so it would not have a Guelph postmark.

"If you keep still," Mother told me, "nobody need ever know. Jean, calm down. It isn't the end of the world."

I did not calm down. I did not fully forgive him until after his death. I did not begin to see how endearing it was of him until I was thirty. I did not tell the story in public until I was forty-five. My fond father was the kind of parent every aspiring writer should be lucky enough to have.

I still had my thirty dollars. I kept looking for exactly the right way to spend it. I saw an advertisement in the *Globe and Mail* for a Great Dane puppy worth thirty dollars. My parents were unmoved by my pleas.

"No Great Dane puppy!" they said in unison.

Buying lots of books tempted me. But I wanted to spend the whole, huge amount on one grand purchase. After all, no eighteen-year-old I knew had thirty dollars to spend in any way he or she saw fit.

Dad tried to get me to start a bank account.

"If you are going to be a writer, you'd better start

learning to use money wisely. You won't have a lot of it."

I had no interest whatever in being practical. I wanted to celebrate.

"No," I said stubbornly. "I don't want to invest it. I want to spend it."

"Do you know what I think you should do with your money?" Mother said suddenly.

"What?" I asked warily, braced to withstand another sensible idea.

"I think you should buy some material, have a dress made, and get Jamie to take you to the At Home," she said.

Was she serious? Why would I want to go to a formal dance with my big brother?

I cringed at the thought of the two or three "tea dances" and class parties I had gone to in grade nine. I had never been asked to dance by a boy. I had only danced with other wallflowers. At the last party I had attended, the well-meaning chaperone had pushed me into a sort of Sadie Hawkins dance. When the music stopped, the person who stood opposite you had to be your partner. The boy opposite me took one look, grimaced and said clearly, "Oh, God, no!" He had then walked off the floor, leaving me deserted. All around me couples had started to dance. Keeping an iron grip on my self-control, I had gone to stand behind the record player. I had stayed there until it was time to go home. I had not been to a dance since.

"I hate dances," I told my mother now.

"But I think this would be different," she said. "You are going to graduate from high school without ever attending a real dance. I don't think your friends would look down on you if Jamie took you. After all, he's a college man. Hugh would be there, too. You could practise dancing with him ahead of time. Think about it."

I thought about it. Betty Hall, Hugh's girlfriend, had become my friend, too. I told her in a joking way what my mother had suggested. She did not laugh. She said I should do it. Both my brothers sounded enthusiastic. Mum and Dad never told me what they had said to make Jamie so courtly. He actually wrote me a letter inviting me to go with him.

When I nervously agreed, Mother and I went shopping for material for my dress. The shop had just gotten in a roll of lustrous, soft green velvet from Paris, France. When they moved it, light shimmered along its folds. I held it up and watched it ripple and gleam. I had never seen anything look so rich. I spent all my Mary and Joseph money on eight yards of it, hoping I was not making a colossal mistake.

The dressmaker made me a lovely dress. There was enough material left to make gloves that stretched from my elbows to two points on the backs of my hands. We also bought a pair of silver sandals.

The night of the dance began to loom ahead like an iceberg. My stomach lurched every time I thought about it.

We pushed the pingpong table out of the way and Hugh and I began to practise dancing. "You're doing fine . . . ouch!" he kept saying. He taught me to waltz and, at the finish, to spin in circles the full length of the pingpong room.

"When the waltz contest is announced, save it for me," he said. "Betty's so short that she falls over my foot when we pivot. You and I pivot perfectly."

On the day of the dance, I had my hair curled. I

wore lipstick and pink nail polish. The dress helped me to feel braver as it slid over my head and settled around me in gleaming folds. When I came down the long staircase, dressed up but inwardly shaking, my brother Jamie stepped forward and handed me a florist's box.

Hugh and Betty were watching. Mum and Dad stood waiting. Mother, as chairman of the board of education, was to be in the reception line with Dad beside her. Pat and Rose were planning to come and look on for awhile from the upstairs gallery that ran around the gymnasium. Grandma was the only one staying home.

I opened the box. Before I saw the gardenia, its heady fragrance reached my nose. I lifted it out with unsteady hands. I had never received a corsage before and had not expected such a thoughtful gesture from my big brother. Feeling shy, I turned to look at him. Had it been his idea or Dad's?

He looked elegant. Debonair, even.

"Thank you," I said uncertainly.

"I had nothing to do with it," my father said, smiling warmly at Jamie.

"Well, I like that!" Jamie pretended to be affronted. "Do you think I don't know how to treat my date?"

I apologized. This was not the brother who, many years before, had dropped me into a creek when he was supposed to be carrying me across it. This was a prince among brothers.

The gym was decorated to look like a huge Valentine. As we waited to go through the heart-shaped gates that let onto the dance floor, I felt a finger run along the rolled collar of my dress.

"It's so soft," a girl whispered. "Feel it."

"I can't," her escort muttered.

"Go on," the girl urged. "She'll never know."

A much heavier finger ran the length of my collar. I felt like giggling. I pretended to have noticed nothing.

When Jamie and I began to dance, I found that Hugh's coaching had worked. I knew what to do with my feet. What's more, I loved doing it. When Jamie asked if I'd like to sit out a dance, I shook my head. Hugh cut in on us and Betty and I changed places.

Mother, Dad, Rose and Pat all went home before the waltz contest was announced. Hugh came to get me.

"1 . . . 2 . . . 3, 1 . . . 2 . . . 3," He was counting in a mutter as we waltzed around the gym.

Couples began to leave the floor as the judges tapped them on the shoulder. We kept dancing. Both of us were counting now. We did not miss a beat. There were only five couples left. Four . . .

"You two are the winners," one of the judges told us, smiling at our astonished laughter. "You were the only couple on the floor doing proper ballroom waltzing."

Up to that moment, the winners of each contest had gone up on stage and been given their prize. They had then done a few steps across the width of the platform. Hugh and I, however, had the entire floor to ourselves.

"Okay, Jean," he murmured, "we'll waltz to the far end. Then, when I give you the signal, we'll pivot."

My heart was pounding. What if I missed the signal? What if I found myself falling over his foot?

We waltzed up to the end. Then, as scattered applause began, Hugh said, "Now, *pivot!*" We were off, spinning around and around, down the entire length of the gym. The applause was real now. As we finished, flushed and laughing, I knew how Cinderella felt dancing with the prince. No wonder she stayed past midnight. I never wanted to go home, either.

When we got home, we woke my parents up so they could see Hugh and me pivot and admire our prize. As we waltzed around their bedroom, careening into the furniture and laughing like idiots, I remembered that my father had wanted me to put my thirty dollars in the bank. If it had lain somewhere collecting interest for forty years, it could never have bought me another such enchanted evening.

And J. A. Alexander knew it.

With Jamie at the dance
(I felt like Cinderella at the ball.)

☧ 23 ☧

I sat near the back in Assembly. I could not see the man on the stage. Yet my attention was riveted on him. He was Wilson Macdonald, the Canadian poet who had written "The Song of the Ski." He was now chanting a poem from his book, *Greater Poems of the Bible*. The students sat mesmerized by his astonishing performance. Nothing like this had ever been heard before at a GCVI Assembly.

> In the beginning, God did make the heavens
> and the earth,
> and the dark sphere was without form, and
> empty
> at its birth;
> and darkness lay in silence on the surface
> of the deep,
> and then His spirit moved across the waters
> in their sleep.
>
> > And God spoke out
> > across the night,
> > "Let there be light,"
> > and there was light.

As Mr. Macdonald spoke forth across our assembled ranks, his voice thundered in a passable imitation of Jehovah's. We knew it was serious, and we were as silent as the deep. But I, for one, felt an uneasy ripple of what came close to laughter, just under the surface of my self-control.

It was hypnotic. But wasn't he almost plagiarizing? And wasn't the original more . . . dignified? Maybe better poetry, even?

"I'm high on the hill and ready to go,/A wingless bird in a world of snow," said a voice inside my head. "The Song of the Ski" had been in our grade seven reader. It seemed wrong to like the swing of it better than this rhyming Genesis. But I did.

Then I reminded myself that I was going to meet this real poet this very afternoon. Dad was bringing him home for a few minutes after he spoke at the Rotary Club.

Would he want to read one of my poems?

Probably not. But it would be wonderful if he did. Which one would I show him?

I made myself listen again to his chanting. After all, he was the first real poet I had ever heard.

When I went home at noon, however, I was so excited that I had trouble eating. Finally we heard them at the front door. Panic-stricken, I turned to Mother. She seemed perfectly calm, as though she met published poets every other day.

"Come on," she told me.

Hiding behind her as much as was possible, since I was inches taller and broader, I followed her out to the hall. Dad, Mr. Macdonald and Mrs. Macdonald were grouped by the door. My father smiled at me. The poet looked tired, elderly and a bit cross. His wife gave us an abstracted glance.

"This is my daughter, Jean," Dad said. "She's the one I was telling you about. She writes poems, too, although she's still just a beginner, of course."

We went into the den. Mr. Macdonald sat down

carefully. He kept his coat on. When he was settled, he looked up at me and held his hand out in mid-air. Humbly, I took it. He held on and gazed at me.

"I like your poems," I said self-consciously. "'The Song of the Ski' was in our grade seven reader."

I felt certain that every word I said sounded stupid and young. I wished he would let go of my hand. He squeezed it instead. He was going to speak. We all waited.

"If you'd take a tablespoonful of blackstrap molasses every morning," he told me in a querulous voice, "your vision would improve markedly. It has helped me so much. One tablespoonful a day!"

"Dear," his wife murmured, trying to head him off, "she has had her condition since birth. It's not the same . . ."

He brushed her words aside with an impatient jerk of his head. He let go of my hand. I put it behind my back.

"It doesn't matter. I'm sure it would do her good," he snapped. "Where's that poem I wrote for White Cane Week?"

His wife obediently produced a white card with a poem printed on it and handed it to me. I took it but did not attempt to read it.

He was ready to go. He had brought his poem to the poor blind girl. He was not interested in the poet. I felt diminished and angry. I also felt cheated. I no longer wanted to show this cranky old man my poems.

Blackstrap molasses, indeed!

As they got him to his feet and started for the door, Dad sent me a look of apology. Mrs. Macdonald avoided my eyes. Her embarrassment was obvious. I felt sorry for her.

The door closed behind them.

I threw the White Cane Week poem down on the hall table. I glared at my mother.

"You have to remember he's an old man," she said quietly. "I imagine the performance at the school and then the speech at Rotary have left him exhausted."

"But did you hear what he said about taking a tablespoonful . . ."

"I heard," Mother said. She started to laugh, both at his ridiculous suggestion and my outraged reaction. After a struggle with myself, I joined in. It was funny, after all.

But was this what poets were like? If so, it was hard to bear.

Then, during the summer between high school and university, Dad made up for this unhappy experience by somehow arranging for me to meet E. J. Pratt.

I sat on the edge of my chair in his office at Victoria College while he read three or four of my poems. He read them carefully, not skimming. He treated me courteously. I had the feeling that to him a nineteen-year-old "poet" was just as real and significant as someone of thirty or forty with a line of published books to her credit. He read the last poem out loud.

> Keats has a gold wing,
> Rich and wide and gleaming.
> Shelley has a bright wing
> Of shining, silver fire.
>
> Rest is in the first wing
> And slow, deep dreaming.
> The other soars amid the stars

In search of heart's desire.

As he read the words quietly, I knew they were all wrong. Why only one wing each, to begin with? You couldn't get off the ground with just one wing. I had written it after studying Keats' "Ode to the Nightingale" and Shelley's "To a Skylark." I had been trying to tell of the sensuous langour I found in the first poem and the mounting exultation in the other. But I hadn't done it. I braced myself for cutting criticism or, even worse, ridicule.

I got neither. Dr. Pratt laid down the sheet of paper, looked at me with kindness, and told me that my poetry "had a sound of Swinburne."

I was ecstatic. I had memorized four lines of a poem by Swinburne, purely because I so loved its sound. Feeling erudite, I shyly recited it.

> In a coign of the cliff, between lowland and
>   highland,
>   At the sea down's edge, between
>   windward and lea,
> Walled round with rocks as an inland island,
>   The ghost of a garden fronts the sea.

Dr. Pratt looked delighted. You would have thought I had done something as astonishing as pulling a live rabbit out of a top hat. He beamed at me. I blushed. I could hardly wait to tell Dad.

"Exactly," said the author of "The Titanic." "You understand just what I mean. But, Jean, you must stop using these contractions. They are an insult to the integrity of the English language. You don't need to say "twixt," "twill," "tween" and so on. If you work a little harder, you can write a better poem without such abominations. Listen."

He read another verse of mine, liberally sprinkled with what I thought were poetic words. Instead of reading the contractions, he read the whole words. The poem was clearly stronger. He was right. I saw I had a lot of rewriting to do. I felt excited at the thought.

"I will never use them again," I said humbly. Then I stood up. Dad was waiting, and I couldn't take up any more of Dr. Pratt's time.

He rose, too, and we shook hands.

"Thank you so much," I said awkwardly, feeling suddenly terribly young again.

"It gave me pleasure," he said gravely. "Keep on writing. We'll hope to see you at Vic one of these days."

I began babbling at my father the instant we were out of earshot of Dr. Pratt's study door.

"He says I write like Swinburne," I told my father inaccurately. "And he told me not to use words like "e're" and "ne'er" any more. You don't need them. They are an insult to the English language. You know, Dad, a language has integrity . . ."

Dad glanced at my shining eyes and smiled. He had done it. He had made me forget the tarnished image of a poet which Wilson Macdonald had left with me.

⚔ 24 ⚔

"Are you quite sure you want to go to university?"
Dad asked me again. "The workload will be heavier
than it was in high school. It would be hard for you to
keep up."

I knew why he was worried. I had almost had to
repeat grade twelve because I had begun making my
poor vision an excuse for not studying. My marks at
Easter shocked even me. Chemistry 31. Physics 24. I
had failed half my subjects. Mr. Hamilton, the principal, had told my parents that if I did not pass in June, I
would have to repeat the year.

"He says you have no self-discipline," Mother
relayed.

"It's not true," I blustered. But I knew it was.

I began to work. I had extra help from my teachers.
In June, I passed every exam.

I did so have self-discipline!

Then Mr. Hamilton advised my parents to have me
take five of my nine grade thirteen subjects one year
and only four the next. If I stuck to two English
courses, two Latin, two French, biology and history, I
could get enough credits to go on to university. He felt
sure I could get in without any math. I would have to.
I had stopped understanding mathematics in grade
nine.

I had had to agree to this one-year-in-two program. I was intent on proving what self-discipline I
possessed. Rarely has one compound word had such
a salutary effect. I passed all nine Departmental exam-

inations. That extra year left me feeling out of step with my contemporaries, though, and I wanted to go to Victoria College and start catching up.

"I just want to try, Dad," I said. "If I find I can't handle it, I'll give up. But first let me try."

The two of us went to Toronto to talk it over with Mr. Woodside, the Registrar of Victoria College. He shook his head over my wish to be admitted to Vic in the English Language and Literature program.

"There is a tremendous amount of reading required for that course," he told me. "Nobody has ever gotten through it with less than normal vision. And your father says you have headaches to contend with as well. Why not register as an occasional student? Then you could attend just the lectures you are interested in. If you audit courses, you won't have to write essays and pass examinations. You don't really want a degree. You want an education."

My father sent me a rueful glance. He knew exactly what I was going to say.

"Couldn't I just try?" I asked. I was not sure myself why it mattered so much. I had no plans that necessitated having a B. A. Yet I stood my ground. "If I find that I can't keep up with the others, I can always drop out. What harm is there in letting me try?"

At the end of a long interview, the three of us rose. I had won. I was going to have my chance. Neither of them believed I was going to make it.

I got a letter to say I was to live in Annesley Hall, one of the women's residences. I got new saddle shoes and pleated skirts. I also got the jitters. I tried to keep my nervousness to myself. After all, going to college was my idea.

Mother planned to come down to Toronto with me

to help me find my way around. She would see to it that I registered for the right classes, knew the layout of the residence and could locate all the places where I would need to go. Knowing she would be there kept my foreboding down to a medium-sized apprehension rather than a full-scale galloping panic. I was even a little excited.

Two days before I was to go, I came down from my attic room in the morning to see a strange green cylindrical object in the hall outside my parents' bedroom. As I paused to stare at it, Mother came out, looking back over her shoulder.

"All right," she called to someone I could not see, "the way is clear."

Something in her voice kept me standing where I was, kept me silent. A great, unreasoning fear made my palms grow clammy.

Then a stranger carrying one end of a stretcher came out into the hall. My father was lying on it.

I stood rooted to the spot as the stretcher bearers carried him to the head of the stairs. Mother went down ahead of them. She had not seen me.

As the second stretcher bearer disappeared, Hugh came out of his room. He was already dressed.

"Dad's had a heart attack, I think," he said in a low, tense voice. "Mum woke me up and sent me to get oxygen for him. But he must have gotten worse, because when I got back with it, she'd already called the ambulance. Come on."

We went downstairs, subdued and anxious, not knowing quite how to behave. Mother went with Dad. The house filled with worry.

Dad had had a severe heart attack. Mother helped me pack for university, but her mind was on that fight for life going on in the Guelph General Hospital.

"I'll be all right on my own," I said.

Mother did not answer.

The night I was to go, she drove me to Toronto. We pulled up in front of Annesley Hall. Light spilled out through the door. Mother helped me out of the car with my suitcase. She hugged me. She looked worried, but she had to get back right away and I knew it. Other girls were going up the steps.

"Jean, I wish . . . I'm sorry, but I can't wait even to see you into your room."

I swallowed hard. I was grown-up, wasn't I? Now was the moment to prove it.

"Go on," I said, giving her a push and picking up my suitcase. "I'll be home on Friday night. Give my love to Dad."

Then, without waiting to watch the car pull away, I marched up the steps and became a Freshman in the class of 5T5.

25

My first week at university was mostly a nightmare, in spite of my new friends.

Sally and Sandy roomed down the hall from me. They were Freshmen, too — friendly, nice girls who did not at all seem to mind being friends with a cross-eyed poet. And a senior was assigned to help me register. She patiently piloted me around the campus, signing me up for my courses. But I missed several meals and classes because I could not find either the dining room or the lecture hall and was too shy to ask. I carried a white cane that first year, but as I found friends to walk with, I stopped using it.

There were get-together dances meant to acquaint the male and female students. I tagged along to a couple and found them to be repetitions of the parties in grade nine. I hated pretending to be enjoying myself when actually I was feeling wretchedly out of place. After the initial weekend was over, I avoided all such functions.

We each had to have an interview with Kathleen Coburn, the acting Dean of Women. She was to become one of my favourite professors. I went in to see her, relieved to have someone to talk with about my overwhelming anxiety about Dad.

She was kindness itself, but before I got up to go, I heard some now familiar words.

"Jean, I don't think you are being realistic when you plan to get through English Lang. and Lit. in just four years. Why not spread the work out over six, if you are set on getting a B. A.?"

I stared at the floor. She made it sound as if only an immature person would not accept such a sensible suggestion.

"I just want to try," I said for what seemed like the millionth time. "The minute that I find I can't handle the work, I'll stop insisting. But what harm can it do to let me try?"

She sighed. I was getting used to hearing that sigh. She was smiling at me.

"Well, it's up to you," she said. "But it's no disgrace to admit the work is more than you bargained for. Come and see me if you're having trouble."

I made it through to Tuesday night. Then Aunt Eva phoned to ask how I was getting along. Before I could tell her, she started to cry. I pressed the receiver so tightly against my ear that it hurt.

"What's wrong?" I demanded.

She gulped and sniffed and then blurted, "I'm so worried about Llew. Gorrie says his lungs are filling up with fluid. I don't think there's much hope."

As soon as she hung up, I called home. Mother was at the hospital. When she returned my call, she sounded so tired.

"Eva shouldn't have upset you," she said. "Your dad is very ill, it's true, but he's still very much himself. Dr. Lewis came from London today to see him. When we came out of his room, Dr. Lewis said, 'Absolutely no visitors except yourself. The silly fool was trying to entertain even me." We both laughed, but our laughter was perilously close to tears.

"I'm not making any promises," she added, "but I think he might surprise us all yet."

"Should I come home?" I asked, willing her to say

yes.

"No," she told me. "There's nothing you can do here. You're job is right there. Llew keeps wondering how you're managing. He's very proud of you."

When I went to visit Dad on Friday evening, I found him still in an oxygen tent. He was clearly very ill. But even so, he had a million questions for me, and I had so much to tell him. As his health slowly improved, I shared all my excitement with him. I had a professor called Northrop Frye who was teaching us a course on the English Bible. It was a Religious Knowledge course, but it was nothing like anything I had heard in church.

"You know what they say about him, Dad?" I quoted one of the Seniors. "In first year you believe in God. In second year you don't believe in God. In third year you believe in Frye's God. In fourth year you believe Frye is God."

Dad's laugh sounded very healthy. I kept talking.

"I think I'm keeping up with everybody else. I read much faster than Sal does. The best thing is, hardly any of the professors write stuff on the board. They just stand up there and talk."

"Are you taking notes?" my father asked.

"Sometimes," I said guiltily. "But if you stop to write, you miss bits. I remember most of what they say."

"Of course, you do have a well-trained memory," Dad said thoughtfully. "Perhaps we were all wrong. I should have guessed that lectures would be the ideal way for you to learn. You may even have an advantage over the rest. How many are in your class?"

"Thirteen," I said. "My first American Lit. essay is due soon."

I finished that first essay confidently. Dad read it before I handed it in. I was almost positive I was the best writer in the class. After all, as far as I knew, not one of them was a poet, let alone one who had had two poems published in *Saturday Night*.

I got a C.

I tried to keep my expression wooden as I looked at that C. I did not want to show the mark to my father. Yet if I didn't, he would be sure to ask. I decided to break the news in a letter. That way I'd escape the lecture.

My strategy failed. His lecture came by return mail.

Dear Jean,

So nice to hear from you and to know that you got a "C." Don't fret about that. The material and presentation were good. It would have made an excellent short filler for a magazine. Mr. McClean is there to *improve* your style. No matter how good we think your writing is, it can be *improved* and a girl from the High School has to realize that and soak up every new idea and be glad to get criticism if it improves your technique.

I feel a great need for improvement in technique in medicine, writing, aye, and in life itself.

Profit from the criticism! Show that you are not resentful but keep the inner spark going.

We are all too inclined to love praise — Grandma worst of all!

The Puritan Past essay, when you read it

over at the end of the year, will sound a bit
flat to yourself — you will yourself think it is
only worth a "C." Wait till you are a lecturer
in English and you'll be critical too, if you are
going to help your students.

love,

Dad

I read it, first with a smile and then with a scowl.
He won a reluctant chuckle from me with the bit
about Grandma. Although my father's health was still
precarious, he sounded so normal in such letters that
instead of being afraid for him, I was highly annoyed.
How dare he call me "a girl from the High School!"

He predicted I'd reread the essay some day and
realize it deserved no better than a C, did he? I got the
paper out and threw it in the wastebasket. Already I
had reread it and already I knew he was right, but I
had no intention of letting him know that.

Throughout the last year and a half of his life, Dad
was far from well. Yet when I came home on week-
ends and told him my latest essay topic, I would
discover a week later that he had read everything he
could unearth on the subject and was prepared to give
me an inquisition. I got so angry at him because he
would not accept my superficial opinions and theories
but pushed me to think things through, to read more
deeply, to spend much more time on each
assignment.

The rest of the family would leave the table and I
would be stuck there, arguing hotly with my father
and resenting his interference. Why did he have to get
involved? Nobody else's father did.

Yet that C was the last one I got in American Lit., and before the year was over, I had the A Dad had bullied me into earning. He never wrote a word for me. He simply needled me into revising my own efforts.

I considered telling him to leave me alone. But he went to so much trouble. He expounded his ideas so eagerly. Perhaps no one else's father cared so much.

"He lives for your visits, Jean," Mother told me.

As he and I wrangled over Pope Innocent III's foreign policy, I thought of the first two lines of the Victoria College song.

> My father sent me to Victoria
> And resolved that I would be a man . . .

My father did not want me to change my sex. All he wanted was to go to university with me.

⚔ 26 ⚔

I made it safely through my first year, final exams and all. I did not say, "I told you so." I had looked at the courses that lay ahead. I had listened to the growling and groaning of the Seniors. I might flunk out yet. But at least people had stopped urging me not to try for a degree.

We moved back to our old house on Woolwich Street that spring. Hugh finished high school and went off to spend a year in Europe, working on a beet farm part of the time and biking around France, Italy and Spain the rest. Jamie was on the point of getting married. Pat, now attending GCVI, was the only one living at home.

I spent much of the summer trying to write my first novel. I wanted to see if I could, in fact, write a book "with chapters." Never having attempted such a feat before, I blithely began by telling the story from nine separate points of view. The major characters included a grandfather, a doctor and his wife, a Dutch girl who worked for them and their several children ranging in age from a college student of nineteen to a mentally retarded six-year-old.

Little Elizabeth's handicap was accepted by her father but not by her mother. The mother did not face the truth until Elizabeth had undergone a nightmare first day at school.

When I carefully typed "The End," the manuscript was 109 pages long. I called it *Let Me Be Gentle*. And, although I had embarked on it as an experiment, I

gazed at that stack of typed pages with intense satisfaction. I had come to love the family I had created. I
was convinced that the entire world would be as fond
of my characters as I was. After all, I had written a
practically perfect book.

Dad was almost as proud of it as I was. He and I
discussed our next step. We decided we would submit
it to McClelland and Stewart.

I had returned to Vic for my Sophomore year when
I got a lovely letter of rejection from Jack McClelland.
He said my book was too short, too chopped up, and
lacked focus. He also said I had talent and should
keep writing.

I was almost as pleased as I would have been had
my manuscript been accepted. I was busy studying. I
had essays due. With only a small sigh, I set the book
aside. I had a sneaking feeling that someday I might
be grateful to Mr. McClelland for turning it down.

In my second year at Annesley Hall.

That winter, my friends were playing basketball in an Inter-house tournament. They thought they were pretty good. They thought they were going to win the championship. They were particularly pleased about this because most of the girls they were to play in the final game were majoring in phys. ed.

Then, on the actual night of the game, their hopes were dashed. One of the Upper Annesley team was away and their spare player grew violently ill just a couple of hours before the game was to begin.

The five hale team members gathered in my room.

"Losing by default!" Sandy wailed. "When the five of us could beat the six of them with one hand tied behind our backs!" (In those days, girls' basketball teams consisted of six, not five, players.)

I had to smile at the image of all these one-handed basketball players triumphing over their opponents. Then I stopped smiling and stared at her. I had had an idea. Should I voice it?

It couldn't hurt. I could pretend I was kidding if they thought it was insane.

"You mean," I said slowly, "that you don't really need a basketball player? All you need is a human being?"

They nodded like a bunch of puppets. They clearly had not gotten the idea. I took a deep breath.

"I'm a human being," I told them.

There was a long moment of total silence while that registered. Then Sally's face lit up.

"Yeah, you're a human being," she cried. "But how . . .?"

It took us awhile to work out our strategy. I would be a menace if I actually attempted to play. If I simply stood still, though, and they played around me, the other team would be confused. We would have a psychological advantage.

When we arrived at the gym, a little giddy and extremely keyed up, I began to have cold feet. I kept quiet about this. After all, I had been the one to make the suggestion. My friends changed into shorts and T-shirts. I stayed in my jeans and sweatshirt. We marched out onto the floor.

The referee looked at us in surprise.

"Oh, you're here," she said. "Somebody just told me you were going to lose by default."

"No," my teammates answered blandly. "We're here."

The referee looked us over.

"Where's your other player?" she asked.

"Jean's playing on our team tonight," Sal said, her voice sounding a possible challenge to battle.

"She can't play," the referee said weakly. "She's blind."

Everybody looked at Sally. "Show us the rule," she said.

The poor referee was so flummoxed that she actually started flipping through the pages of her little book. She did not find a rule stating that blind people were not allowed to play basketball.

"Come on, Jean," Sandy said, turning to action. "Here's your spot."

She led me onto the floor and positioned me in the centre of one end of the basketball court. My friends ran around, warming up, taking practice shots at the basket.

The other team was standing in a small clump, staring at me. I pretended to be unaware of them.

"We're ready whenever you are," Judy called to

them.

Suddenly I found myself in the middle of bedlam. Nobody who has not stood immobile in the middle of a basketball game without being able to follow what is happening, can have a clear idea of how terrifying it is. The noise is deafening. You feel sure that any second somebody is going to knock you flat. I bit my lip and kept still, waiting for them to trample me to death.

My guard did her best. For a good five minutes she leaped up and down in front of me, waving her arms like a windmill. I grinned at her and continued standing still.

It did not cross her mind that seeing how little threat I was, she should have deserted me and given her team some much-needed support. She was, as we had foreseen, psychologically at a disadvantage. She did finally begin to flag, though. Her hands went to half mast and ended up merely twitching. But she stayed with me, just in case I was up to something.

We got a basket. We got two. My team was playing brilliantly.

At halftime, we were ahead. Everybody but me was hot and triumphant. They mopped their sweaty brows. I was not at all hot. We all went and sucked oranges. I was not thirsty, either, but I was companionable.

Their team was talking hard and fast to my guard. My team glanced over at the poor thing and snickered.

"We're going to win hands down," Judy said.

"Yeah," the others agreed, juice on their chins, the light of battle in their eyes.

I was escorted to the other end of the court. I took

up my position and tried to look as though I had some secret weapon up my sleeve. But they were onto us now. The whistle blew. Bodies hurtled by. Shouts bounced off the walls. I wanted to shut my eyes and cover my ears. I did neither. Basketball players don't.

My guard was ignoring me completely now. They got more baskets. The score mounted up. We were nearly at the end of the game. And it was tied.

Then, for the first time since the game began, I saw the ball. It was sailing by me at about chest level. I had no idea who had thrown it or who was ready to catch it.

I could take that ball, I thought, and, reaching out both hands, plucked it out of the air.

The game came to an abrupt standstill. The blind girl had the ball. Nobody, least of all the blind girl, had any idea what to do next. People froze. Silence fell.

"Jean," Sally yelled, coming to her senses, "throw it here!"

I could not see her, but I could hear her shout. Obediently I sent the ball flying toward that voice. Sal grabbed it and tossed in the basket. The whistle blew. The game was over. We had won!

We laughed like idiots all the way home.

The next time I went to Guelph, I regaled the family with this tale of heroism. Mother, who had played basketball, laughed. Dad laughed so hard I thought he'd choke. Pat looked shocked. She was still in high school and trying to conform.

But Dad soon switched the conversation back to the essay I was writing. I was to discuss whether ~~Samuel~~ Alexander Pope's ~~Johnson's~~ words, "The proper study of Mankind is Man," ~~and tell how they related to his own life and~~ could be applied to the life and writings of Samuel Johnson."

~~writing.~~ I told Dad my theories. He thought I was all wrong. He produced a book about the good doctor called *Mr. Oddity.*

"Before you finish that essay, I want you to read this," he said.

I took it unwillingly. It had 333 pages. I already knew all I needed to know. Why did I have to read another long bookful of the same stuff?

Irritated and determined not to read a word of it, I took the book back to Vic with me. I found myself eyeing it. I liked the title. I'd just glance through it. I stayed up till after midnight reading all the way to the end.

Dad was right.

Damn!

I threw out the pages I'd written and began over again. When I finished, I'd let Dad read it. He'd know then that I had discovered he was right.

On Thursday night I phoned home. I decided to call Mother person-to-person. Otherwise I might end up talking to Grandma.

Dad answered. When the operator said it was a person-to-person call for Dr. Flora Little, he called her to come to the other phone. Before he hung up, though, he said, "Jean, I know you want to talk with your mother. But I wanted to tell you that I'm going into the hospital tomorrow for a little surgery."

"Is it serious?" I asked, startled and unsure what to say.

"I don't expect so," Dad said. "But I just thought I'd tell you. How's the essay coming?"

I did not want to admit over the telephone that he had been right. I wanted him to find out by reading my essay.

"I'll let you read it when I get home," I said. "Then you can see for yourself."

"Well, you wanted to talk to your mother. Here she is." I started to say I'd talk with him, too. I could hear hurt in his voice, but he had already hung up.

"He says he's going to the hospital," I said to Mother.

"Yes."

"He says it's nothing serious."

I heard no unusual tension in her voice as she reassured me. I did not know enough to be concerned that someone with so damaged a heart was having to undergo an anaesthetic.

I got a letter from Dad the next morning. I chuckled at his fancy turn of phrase as I went up the stairs to my room. He called Mother's birthday her "festival." I was still smiling when I pushed open my door.

Elizabeth Kerr, who was now Elizabeth Pearson, was there sitting on my bed. I was amazed and pleased. She was one of my favourite people. She came to read to me sometimes, but I was not expecting her.

"What are you doing here?" I asked.

She did not answer. She got up and came toward me. She took me in her arms. She was weeping.

"What has happened to you?" I asked, appalled.

Then, as she still did not speak, I felt a huge coldness spreading through me.

"Or has something happened to me?" I said through stiff lips.

"Jean, your mother asked me to come and tell you," she said, her voice thick with tears. "Your dad's gone."

⚚ 27 ⚚

I drew back carefully. I knew that making a sudden movement might break the fragile shell of unreal calm in which I had instantly taken shelter. I could not let the truth of what she had said reach me.

I glanced around the room for something to do. I clutched a sheet of paper in my right hand. Dad's handwriting leaped up at me.

> It was quite true that your pen was dipped in *Mr. Oddity's* ink pot . . . . When I read the book, I felt that there was a certain human greatness about the man. He seems to have left a record of blunt scholarliness . . . . I am looking forward to reading the finished product. I only wish it were possible for you to read more of what he wrote himself and less of what others wrote *about* him . . .

"But he wrote to me." I showed her. "He can't . . ."
Elizabeth's eyes held such pity that I turned away and walked over to the window. It was a glorious day. The sky was a brilliant blue without a wisp of cloud.

As I stood there, she told me that Dad had died in the operating room without regaining consciousness. His heart had simply given up.

"Your Uncle Bill is coming to get you and your aunt," she went on. "Can I help you pack?"

I began to put things into a suitcase. I felt I was behaving rationally. Why wasn't I crying? I wondered dully if I were unnatural. When I unpacked, however, I found a belt to a dress that I had left in Toronto, two mismatched shoes, a blouse with no cufflinks.

When I was ready to go, it was nearly noon. As I sat waiting for my uncle, somebody brought me a sandwich. I felt ashamed when the food tasted good.

Jessie Macpherson, the Dean of Women came in and said quietly how sorry she was. I had never learned the manners of bereavement. I said something inane about it not mattering. Her startled expression, lasting only an instant, brought the truth one step nearer. Then she gently touched my hand and left me with my friends.

Pat came with Uncle Bill and Aunt Eva. The two of us sat in the back seat. It was such a relief to have her there. We kept giggling over nothing. Dad's brother and sister, who did not hear the tears in our laughter, were silent and disapproving. When we reached home, our house was cluttered with people. The next-door neighbour mopped her streaming eyes and patted my unresponsive shoulder.

"Poor dear," she wept.

I kept my head down and brushed past. Why were all these people here? They turned to stare. I looked around desperately for somewhere to hide.

Then Aunt Mary, Uncle Bill's wife, grabbed me by the arm and, never loosing her grip, propelled me to where Mother was standing surrounded.

"Here's your mother, dear," she announced and let go.

Ever since Elizabeth had told me the news, I had been longing to get to my mother. I wanted to be taken into her arms, to be comforted and to comfort in return, to share some of my overwhelming fear and need.

But everyone was watching.

"Hi, Mum," I said.

"Hi," she returned.

We exchanged a stiff embrace, the kind one can exchange in public. And I hated the interlopers with all a child's fierce passion.

Although I had just had my twenty-first birthday two months before, I learned right then how death can strip away one's maturity and uncover the desolate child underneath.

Jamie and his new wife Pat came from Kingston. Yet the hurt of the next few days was intensified by the fact that we were unable to reach Hugh. He was biking through Spain and did not learn of Dad's death till a week later when Mother's telegram finally caught up with him.

I discovered then how close laughter is to tears, how family jokes bound us to each other, how grief is not realized all at once, but comes to you little by little.

When I went back to school a week later, I chose my essay topic for Frye's course on Milton — "The Concept of Liberty as Shown in Milton's Prose." It sounded daunting, but then so did all the others.

In Guelph the following weekend, I said to my family, "I have to write an essay on Milton's concept of liberty."

They went on eating. "That sounds like a challenge," Mother said encouragingly. The phone rang. It was time to clear the table. As I got up to remove the plates, the conversation turned to other things.

I sat back down. I stared fixedly at the helping of rice pudding Pat passed to me.

But the shell had broken at last. I knew Dad had died. Nobody was going to read Milton's prose and be ready to argue with me the next time I came home. If I got a good mark, they would be glad. But nobody here would be waiting eagerly to read what I had written.

Why hadn't I realized before what Dad had done for me? Why had I never told him how much his criticism and encouragement meant?

I had gotten an A on my Samuel Johnson essay. Why hadn't I told him that on the phone, and that I had rewritten it?

If only I had known.

I began to try to write a poem about him, what made him special, how much I loved him. By the time I had finished it, it was over one hundred lines long. As I worked at polishing it, I felt guilty about turning grief into poetry. Yet two of the lines, referring to another girl's pain, said it best. And it didn't matter that she was a made-up girl, grieving for a fictional father.

> I know now why the dazed Ophelia cried
> That violets withered when her father died.

I became a Junior.

During the Christmas holidays, ten months after Dad's death, I grew mysteriously ill. I ran a low fever daily and felt like Emily Bronte. Mother sent me for tests.

I did not have hepatitis. I did not have mononucleosis. I was not anaemic. I continued to have a fever. I remained in bed. January passed. February went by. Halfway through March, Mother came into my room one afternoon and sat on the edge of my bed.

"Jean, I'm afraid you are going to have to let your class go on without you," she said gently. "I don't see any possibility of your getting well in time to do the assignments you've missed and pass your exams."

I stared at her. It had never crossed my mind that I would not graduate with the rest. I had to pass. I couldn't let Mr. Woodside and Miss Coburn be right.

I began to swing my feet out of bed.

"Where are you going?" Mother asked.

"Back to school," I told her through gritted teeth.

The first time I climbed the two flights of stairs to my residence room, I had to sit down halfway to catch my breath. When I got to my room, I wrote out on a piece of paper the fifty-nine things I still had to read. I had thirty-eight days to get through them all. I drew a small box beside each title and coloured them in as I finished. I stayed up all one night skimming *Tom Jones*. The only box I did not colour in was the one next to *Humphrey Clinker*.

When I got third-class honours, I could hear Dad cheering.

In my last year, I took ten English courses. Several of us, however, discovered that while the students in the three-year general course were offered a course in Canadian literature, we honours English students were given no such option. We went to Northrop Frye, the chairman of the English department, to register our indignation.

He looked us over, smiling very slightly at our outrage. Then he said that if we wanted to come to his office a couple of times a week, he would be glad to give us some lectures on the subject. We would get no credit, of course, but he would be pleased to teach us. I doubt that we fully realized what a privilege those lectures were.

As I prepared for the final examinations, one night I got sidetracked reading Robert Browning. I happened on a wonderful long poem that the professor had never mentioned, "Bishop Bloughram's Apology." I was so excited by it that I vowed to read it again often. While I had the book open, I started "The Ring and the Book." I read the first Book and then skipped to the finish. It was too long to bother with.

I typed my exams in Mr. Woodside's office, where there was a good light. As I looked over the Victorian poetry examination, I was horrified. Many of the poems were unfamiliar to me. If I had not read Bishop Bloughram, I would not have been able to answer a whole section. I would have to use my scant knowledge of "The Ring and the Book," too. This would not be easy, since our professor had not even lectured on these poems.

When, weary and worried, I came out of Vic, I found my entire class assembled outside Annesley waiting for me.

"We've written a petition," Allen said, "and we're waiting to get your signature. Then we're taking it to Frye."

"What sort of petition?"

"Explaining why none of us could write those two Browning questions."

I felt my face go pink. I avoided their eyes.

"But I did answer the questions," I said.

There was a stunned silence.

"How could you have?" Allen demanded. "We'd never been asked to read the poems."

I squirmed under his accusing stare.

"I didn't read all of 'The Ring and the Book,' " I said in my own defence. "But I did read 'Bishop Bloughram's Apology.' I'm sorry. I just . . . really like Browning."

My class got up in a body and left me without a word. We never learned the fate of the petition. Yet when the results came out and I stood at the head of the Vic students in English Lang. and Lit., I wondered if I had Bishop Bloughram to thank.

Graduation Day was heady. After I had gone up and been presented with my diploma, a young man went forward in a wheelchair. The Chancellor came down from the platform to bestow his degree on him. Then the audience rose in a standing ovation. I stood up, too, clapping with everyone else. But I felt miffed. I should have carried that white cane.

In the evening there was a reception at Victoria College for the graduates of 5T5. As I stood there amid a throng of friends and parents, Mr. Woodside and Miss Coburn came up to me. I looked into their smiling eyes.

"Jean, we just wanted to tell you that we now know how mistaken we were," said Mr. Woodside. "We're glad that you've proved us wrong."

I tried to look modest, but it was hard. I could feel my grin stretching from ear to ear. When I was a Freshman, Dad had written wistfully:

> Originally, I had hopes that you would "bust the record" — Now I am far more sensible — For you, all that I crave is the joy of sharing in the life of the University and the fine group of friends you have made at Annesley Hall. You have excelled far beyond my

expectations and, if you continue as you are doing, there can be little doubt about you going on into the second year.

I'd done better than that. I had come fourth in English Language and Literature and first in the list of second class honours. And I'd done it in four years! Even my father must be satisfied.

Yet inside my head I could hear him say, "Jean, next time, read 'The Ring and the Book,' too."

✲ 28 ✲

I wanted to be a writer. But I had been told over and over again that you could not make a living as a writer. You had to get a real job and write in your spare time.

But what real job could a legally blind girl with a B. A. in English do?

Then I learned that the Rotary Crippled Children's Centre planned to start a small class for handicapped children and would need a teacher for it. I had no teaching qualifications, but I had worked with children with motor handicaps for three summers at Woodeden Camp.

The Rotarians agreed to hire me if I would first go to Montreal for two weeks to take a course on educating children with motor handicaps. The course was taught by Ellen Thiel from the Institute for Special Education at the University of Utah in Salt Lake City. I was intimidated by the other students, most of whom were experienced teachers and, although I enjoyed the course itself, I decided I would have to give up the idea of being a teacher. They kept talking a language I did not understand. Phonics, for instance. It was clearly of paramount importance, and I did not know what it meant. When I went in for my final interview, I explained all this to Ellen.

She laughed. "Phonics notwithstanding, I think you just may be a born teacher. I'm about to give a six-week course in Salt Lake on teaching children with motor handicaps. How would you like to come home to Utah with me and we could find out if I'm right?"

I stared at her, not knowing for a second whether or not she was kidding. Then I saw her grin. It was very friendly and had in it the same challenge that Dad's had had so often.

"All right," I said dazedly. "Where's Utah?"

I called home half an hour later to tell Mother that I was coming home to pack tomorrow and, the day after, was meeting this strange woman, Ellen Thiel, in Urbana and setting out for the American West.

"Wonderful," Mother said after only the shortest of hesitations. "I'll be there to meet you. You can tell me all about it while we pack."

At the end of that summer, I made a list in my diary of all the "new experiences" I had had since I left home. There are forty-nine items listed. I stopped only because I had filled the last page in that diary.

I did discover what Phonics meant, but I learned far more than that. The children in the demonstration class taught me a lot. So did Ellen's three children, Paula, Mary and Joe.

One evening I was reading *The Secret Garden* to the Thiel kids. Paula and Mary were enthralled by the story, but Joe kept fiddling with odds and ends on his bed and behaving as though he were extremely bored. When I closed the book, however, and started to shepherd the girls out of his room, he demanded that I give him the phone.

"Why?" I asked. "It's time you went to sleep. I read two extra chapters because the girls were so interested."

"I have to tell Mama something," Joe said.

Ellen was working late at the university. But I knew

she was alone and besides, who was I to come between a boy and his mother?

I handed him the telephone on its long cord. Returning after tucking in the girls, I heard him say in a voice filled with wonder and delight, "Mum, they got into the garden!!!"

Never again did I make the mistake of thinking that a child who appeared inattentive was getting nothing out of a book. His tone held exactly the joy Mary Lennox herself felt when she stepped through the ivy-covered green door.

At the end of the summer, Ellen wrote me a glowing letter of recommendation, and I went back to Guelph to start preparing for my teaching job at the Crippled Children's Centre.

I was not an ideal teacher. When your students continually correct your arithmetic, it keeps you humble. But I did one important thing well. I read to them.

I found that these were deprived children, not because they were not loved, but because they had largely been kept indoors due to their handicaps. Not one of them had ever seen a rainbow or been to a circus. They could not swim. They had not been taken to a zoo. Most of them had not ridden on a city bus. None had been on a train journey. Most had never eaten in a restaurant.

We did all these things, and Phonics, too.

Remembering how I had never found a cross-eyed heroine in a book, I decided to search for books about children with motor handicaps. I did not for one moment intend to limit my students to reading about crippled kids. I knew that they completely identified with Anne Shirley and Homer Price, that they actually became Bambi, Piglet and Wilbur. I did not think they needed a book to help them adjust. I did believe, however, that crippled children had a right to find themselves represented in fiction.

I began to search.

I found a book about a girl with polio. None of my students had polio. The Salk vaccine had already been discovered. I found several books that contained invalid children who completely recovered before the book ended. None of my students was ever going to recover completely.

I was looking for a book in which the child's handicap was present only in the background. The kids I taught were not conscious of their disabilities most of the time. They minded when people stared at them, or when their brothers and sisters got bicycles, of course. But usually they were too busy living to brood. Physio and occupational therapy were like arithmetic and reading, an accepted part of their days.

When we read *The Secret Garden*, Alec said, "What's the matter with Colin? Why doesn't he have therapy?"

"I guess it was written too long ago for them to know about therapy," I said weakly.

"What I can't figure out," Clifford complained, "is how he stood up for the first time in June and was well enough to beat Mary in a race by August. That's crazy."

The others loved the ending so much that they defended Colin's rapid recovery. But even they sounded a bit dubious.

We went through the same questions when we read *Heidi*. Clara got well even faster than Colin.

"Miss Little, what was wrong with Clara?"

It didn't say. I began to feel angry on their behalf.

Why couldn't there be a happy ending without a miracle cure? Why wasn't there a story with a child in it who resembled the kids I taught?

Somebody should write one, I thought.

It did not yet cross my mind that that somebody might be me.

✖ 29 ✖

I returned to Salt Lake that summer to learn more about teaching. When I faced the children in September, I felt a little more confident. I still read aloud to them every day.

"I thought you were supposed to teach *them* to read," one of the therapists remarked acidly.

"Why would they want to learn if they'd never had a joyful experience connected with reading?" I asked.

She had not been present when I had handed a new student a book only to have him burst into tears and refuse to take it.

"I can't read," he had sobbed. "I've failed grade one three times."

I had put the book away and taught him to read by having him trace words he wanted to write. He soon could manage *The Cat in the Hat*. But he wanted to be able to read books like *The Secret Garden*.

I planned to go back to Utah to take further courses. Then Ellen wrote me about a summer course in creative writing which was also being offered at the university. Perhaps I would be interested in attending it as well.

I had never heard of the guest writers, but I was interested. I signed up for some lectures by a novelist named Virginia Sorenson. She had written several books for adults and had just won the Newbery Medal for her children's novel, *Miracles on Maple Hill*.

Virginia Sorenson radically changed my life. First of all, I sat and took in the fact that she was not male, dead or English. If she could get her work published, there was hope for me.

But I was not ready to write a novel yet. I took my Education courses and went on teaching. In my spare moments, though, I read everything of Virginia Sorenson's that I could lay my hands on. All of her books moved me, but the one that affected me the most was her Newbery winner.

The heroine was real. So were her parents. When I read how upset Marly was over her father killing some baby mice, I remembered a summer long ago when we had been holidaying in Muskoka. A skunk had taken refuge under one of the cabins, and my father and brothers had helped the proprietor shoot it. I had never before really hated my father, but that day I did.

You could put the raw pain of such a day into a story. It would help children to feel less alone if they could read about such moments. You could also put in times of joy or self-discovery.

Then, one noon hour, as I sat eating lunch with the children, one of them told me about an unhappy experience she had had the night before. She and her older sisters had gone to filch some apples from a neighbour's tree.

"She set her dog on us," the child related in a trembling voice. "The others ran but I tripped and fell and the dog jumped right on top of me. That was a terrible thing she did, wasn't it, Miss Little?"

Before I could answer, the other children jumped

in.

"You were stealing!" they told her. "Stealing's wrong. They were her apples."

The child sat silent for a long moment. Then she raised her troubled eyes to mine and said, "But, Miss Little, my mother sent me with a basket."

I gave her a hug. I could not do much else. She would have to forgive her mother herself.

Yet the incident haunted me. Somebody should write a book about children like her, I thought, real children.

When school ended, I decided to take time off to get properly trained as a teacher. I tried first to get admitted to teachers' college in Ontario, but I failed the medical examination. Ellen then managed to get me into the course offered by the University of Utah. I had to promise that I would not try to get a job in the state. Then I had to pass. In one year I had a teacher's certificate.

"But I don't want to go back to teaching quite yet," I told Ellen. "I want to try to write a book first."

I sat down at my typewriter.

"Sal Copeland was scared," I typed.

Sally Copeland had cerebral palsy. Like me, she had a West Highland white terrier called Susie. She cheated on a mental arithmetic test on her first day in grade five. She was afraid she would have no friends.

At the end of the story, Sal was still walking on crutches, still wearing braces. But she had grown from a scared, lonely outsider into a dog lover and good friend.

As I wrote and rewrote the book, I felt a delight I

had not known since I had worked on *Let Me Be Gentle* when I was twenty. I moved right into the world where Sally lived and I thought I held the fates of all the characters in my hands. Except that before I was through, they began doing things I had not planned. They kept surprising me. I loved that.

I had written a book. It was different from *Let Me Be Gentle,* because I had intended the first for my family and friends and only afterwards wondered if it were publishable. This one I had written purposely for strangers to read. I had worked much harder and longer on it. It was done. Now what?

I went to the Children's Library. When I told Dorothy Metcalfe my problem, she brought me the rules for the Little Brown Canadian Children's Book Award.

"It can't hurt to try," she said.

I mailed the manuscript to the contest just before the deadline. Then I tried to concentrate on teaching. After all, Little Brown would not announce the winner till May.

That fall, Grandma grew ill. I would come home from school and sit with her. She liked me to sing. I came to know all her favourite hymns by heart. I also read her my manuscript. I'm not sure that she heard much of it, but she told me it was very nice. The children at the Centre liked it, too. Janice said, "Sal Copeland is me!" She was not, but I was pleased. Perhaps other children would feel that way, too.

Grandma died that December. As April neared its end, I gave my family specific instructions.

"If a fat envelope comes from Little Brown," I told

them, "don't phone the school. It'll be the manuscript sent back to me. But if I should by any chance get a *thin* letter, telephone and I'll come right home."

Pat, my sister, was helping me at the school the day the phone rang.

I stopped mixing more red poster paint for Paddy Brown and moved quickly into the hall to where the phone sat, shrilling its summons.

"Beechwood School," I said.

"Jean, come home. It's a thin letter!"

I hung up and turned to Margaret Bryant, the teacher's aid and receptionist.

"It's a thin letter," I said. "I'll be back as fast as I can."

As Pat and I went out the door, I heard an indignant voice protesting, "Miss Little, I'm waiting for my paint!"

I did not even glance back. Margaret would take care of it. Pat and I were in the car speeding toward home. As we approached the train tracks at Edinburgh Road, the guard rail went down and a train began to move slowly across in front of us.

I groaned.

"We might as well wait," Pat said. "If we try to go around it, it'll take even longer."

Steam hissed. The train came to a halt. Then, ponderously, it began to reverse.

I couldn't believe it. Pat groaned with me this time.

Finally it was out of our way, and we shot across the tracks. As we pulled up in front of the house, I jumped out of the car and ran.

It's a letter of rejection, I tried to prepare myself.

232 • Jean Little

Or, *maybe*, a letter to say I didn't win the prize but they still want to publish the manuscript.

Mother held the envelope out to me. I grabbed it, ripped it open and then deliberately slowed myself down. If it were bad news, why hurry? If it were good news, prolong the moment.

I eased the top of the letter out and looked at the first line of print.

Dear Miss Little,

I am writing to tell you we want to publish your novel *Mine for Keeps* and . . .

I quit reading and let out a shriek. I thrust the letter at Mother, crumpling it badly in my excitement.

"It says they want to publish it!" I yelled at her, though she stood right in front of me. "I'm going to have a book published."

"Read the rest, you goose," Mother told me.

I pulled the whole sheet of paper out and looked at the next sentence.

. . . if you are willing to work with our Children's Editor Helen Jones on some revisions, we want to give you the award of $1,000.00.

The letter was signed J. G. McClelland, the same Mr. McClelland who nine years before had told me to keep writing.

I handed it back to Mother, feeling as though I might burst. I watched her face light up even more as she read the incredible words. We were both intensely happy. I hugged her violently, and then drew away long enough to speak.

"If it really comes true," I said, "I'm going to dedicate it to Dad."

A picture of me with my dog, Susie *(I had the picture taken to use on the back cover of* Mine for Keeps.)